The Christmas (
Volume Or

By G. Lawrence

Copyright © Gemma Lawrence 2016
All Rights Reserved.
No part of this manuscript may be reproduced without
Gemma Lawrence's express consent

This book is dedicated to my father, who, as a responsible leader on a Woodcraft camping trip decided to dress up like a zombie-ghost and scare everyone into an overexcited frenzy...

And to my sister, for her tales of the killer sheep of Dartmoor...

Guardian

I was lost.

There was no point in trying to deny it now. There was no other person in the car to witness my discomfiture at having to relinquish that last vestige of male pride which states that we *always* know where we are in a car, as though we have some sort of satellite map system attached to the Y chromosome. Since I was alone in this car, I only had to admit the truth to myself, but even that was hard enough.

I was, indeed, lost.

The wipers on the car moved sluggishly against the falling snow. Outside there was only the black night's sky and the barren yet bleak beauty of Bodmin Moor to witness my navigational failure. The snow had been falling for more than an hour as the car climbed upwards and upwards through the winding and often, it seemed, (to a city dweller such as myself) ridiculously small tracks which covered the moors. I would not call them roads, for there was barely enough space to move two cars past each other; something which the locals I had infrequently passed on the lower tracks of the moor seemed to put to the test with more courage than I had, sliding their cars past me and making me cringe each time it happened. But now I had not seen another car for a long time. A long time. And I seemed to have passed all vestiges of civilisation too.

I looked glumly on the moor as I drove; it was beautiful, and had I not been overwhelmed with a sense of my own helplessness, I might have been more impressed. Might have spent time musing in a poetic manner over the rugged stony outcrops and tors, the prickled bushes of gorse and the rising and falling lumps of the land before me, which were gradually being covered in glittering snow.

Spending Christmas up here, in the middle of nowhere, had not been my idea. My fiancée, Billie, had the thought about a month ago, when we were deciding on whose family to spend the holiday with. With my family there was always the risk of being overwhelmed by my mother's love and concern, which more often came out of her mouth as doubt-ridden emphasis on my supposed inability to do anything. My mother was what I had seen teenagers refer to as a *naysayer* on social media; a person who doubted each and every thing I attempted, but did it in a manner that seemed as though all she wanted was for me to be happy. She was a master at it, and such a master at instilling it within me that for weeks after a visit home, I could be relied on to still carry with me the heaviness of her lack of belief that I could accomplish anything, no matter what evidence there was to the contrary. She had done it when I said I wanted to set up my own business, she had done it when I told her I had found the girl I loved... in all things, my mother had *doubt*, and it was as infectious as it was demoralising. At Billie's house, in the USA, was a family of almost puritanical fastidiousness. In sharp contrast to our own flat in London, pure white carpet lined the rooms and corridors, matching the pure white of the sofas and chairs... and there was always the chance that one might spill a drop of wine or drop a crumb on the floor, leading to immense anxiety and remorse for the rest of the visit, and a complete inability to relax. We had found a common bond in our mutual amusement and despair at our families, as we had found bonds in many other ways.

So it was as we sat, heavy-hearted and wondering what to do; how to visit both of the households within the time we had off from work, which was clearly impossible, seeing as we only had a few days, or wondering if we should visit one this year and the other the next, that the love of my life had had her brilliant (or so it appeared at the time) wheeze on what to do instead.

"We should take a trip ourselves," she said, looking at me with that light of sudden inspiration she often had, which both attracted me to her, and which I sometimes despaired at. Whenever Billie had a new thought, a new hobby, it became her *life*. She was set on every new thing with a determination, and a belief in herself which I found quite breathtaking… until she tired of it and left it behind. It had not been the same with all the things she brought into our lives in this way; despite the difficulties, she had continued to learn the guitar and was rather good at it now, and her sudden enthusiasm for painting in acrylics had never dimmed, but all the same, there were an awful lot of abandoned hobbies and callings gathering dust in our attic space.

"We should go somewhere, just the two of us, and have a Christmas together," she went on, her pretty brown eyes lighting up with a sparkle.

"We'd have *both* the families put out with us then, wouldn't we?"

Billie shrugged, "one or the other has to be unhappy anyway, we don't have enough time to visit both this Christmas, not with you working until the twenty-fourth."

"I can't get out of it," I said defensively, jumping over the words.

"I *know* that," she reminded me with the kind of chilly calm which secretly says *stop going on about it*, so well recognised by those in long-term relationships; we speak to each other in code, and give warnings to avoid fights in our tones…

"Well? What do you think?"

"About what?"

She sighed at me, "about us *going away*? Think about it, we could go somewhere where… just you and me. Rent a cottage… we could take all the food and just hole up somewhere for a few days, play board games, watch old movies, go out for walks in the snow and snuggle up with a glass of wine in the evenings… it would be great!"

"Walks in the snow?" I asked with a laugh, "this is England; if we're lucky we might have a touch of frost on Christmas morning."

"Scotland?" she asked, picking up her wine glass and swirling the crimson fluid around in it thoughtfully, "up in the highlands?"

"It would take days to drive up there," I replied, putting down the idea, but starting to warm to the principle in general, "and if we went on the train the tickets would cost more than the hire of a cottage… or to *buy* a cottage in fact…"

She laughed. "Well, where else might it snow in the UK then, which isn't too far away?"

I drained my glass and got up, slightly unsteadily, to fetch the bottle; a Friday night in, when I had got home at a reasonable hour was a rare thing for a manager of a busy restaurant. Most of the time, I had to be there *all* the time, and as the place got more and more successful, the more work and the more hours it seemed to demand of me. That was why I had to work until the twenty-fourth… late bookings, staff needing to leave for holidays… I had started the place myself, and worked almost every role in the place over the years, but even now, I had to be all things to all men when I walked through its doors. It earned me a good wage now, after many years of dog-hard work, and I loved the place, I was proud of it, but that didn't mean I didn't like a moan about it at times. I am British after all; moaning is our national pastime. I came back to the table with the wine and topped up our glasses.

"You'd need somewhere up high," I said, "like the moors, Yorkshire or something."

"That's also pretty far north," she mused, looking at her wine again.

"There's moors in Cornwall and Devon," I suggested, "I don't think snow could be guaranteed, but there's a better chance there than anywhere else."

She looked up at me with happy eyes. "How long would that take to get there?" she asked; my American immigrant girlfriend, who came over here to take jobs away from British people, of course, and never seemed to know where anything was in the UK despite living here for four years. I smiled at her.

"I'm going to get you a road map of the UK for Christmas," I teased, "and test you on it." I ducked to avoid her playful cuff about my head, and laughed, "peace, Yanke, peace!"

"I'm not from New England, ignorant limey," she grinned at me. "Cornwall… as in, *Rebecca* and *Jamaica Inn*, Cornwall?" I could see she was interested already. I wasn't surprised. Our small two-bedroom flat in Kingston was stuffed with books; paperbacks and hardbacks, fiction and non-fiction, biography and fantasy. Billie *devoured* books; there was no other way of saying it. It was as though she needed them as avidly as she needed food, water or air. The rate at which Billie read was always fascinating to me. I was a slow reader at best. When we first met I generally assumed that she was skim-reading, but then her knowledge of every book she had read astounded me. She had a much better memory than me, and always seemed to seek the meaning behind the written words on the page. Billie read upwards of one to two hundred books every year, *and* worked full time as an accountant, *and* helped me with my accounts, *and* helped out at a dog rescue centre every other Saturday… her energy was astounding. And I could see by the look in her eyes that she was interested for sure now… to get to wander the paths which might lead her to Manderley again… to tramp over the moors where Jem the horse thief might still lurk… it was like a dream to her.

"It might not snow though," I warned her.

"But there's a chance, right?"

"There's a chance."

And there, that Friday night over the last dregs of the bottle of wine, with take-out containers from my restaurant stacked to one side of us, we'd trawled through cottages available for rent at Christmas on the moors, in Cornwall. It was late to be booking, even in early November, but we found a few we could afford. The one we decided upon was a quaint old farmer's cottage out in the middle of Bodmin Moor; quite removed from what I would deem as civilization, but there was a village about a mile from the cottage, with a pub, which we thought might well be good for a wintry walk to, and have a pint of some fondly-imagined local ale delicacy. The cottage itself had one bedroom and looked well-maintained. There was even an open fire which Billie squeaked over with glee when we looked over the pictures online. We figured that Billie could come down a day or so before me in her car, bringing most of the food with her, and start to make the place 'homely', as she called it, for our Christmas break. I would get away on Christmas Eve, after lunch service, and drive straight down, a five-hour trip, but hopefully a worthwhile one, and join her by that evening. She promised to have a roaring fire ready and a bottle of good wine decanted for us to drink next to the fire. We had gone over and over our plans with almost childlike glee, and I had barely even felt the guilt which my mother slathered on me when I called to let her know that we would not be joining the other Andersons for Christmas that year.

"You're abandoning me," she sighed down the phone, and I could almost see her expression of self-induced martyrdom as she spoke.

"Not really, Mum," I replied, keeping the image of the little cottage and the roaring fire in my mind as a kind of buffer against my mother's insistence of my guilt. "It's only one year, after all, and you'll have Jenny, Lee and the kids over, won't you?"

"It might be difficult to find the cottage," said my resident naysayer, "and you never know what could happen, so far out of the way…"

"We'll be fine, Mum," I sighed a little, feeling her infectious doubt seeping from the phone and into my fingertips. "And it would be nice for Billie and me to spend some time together. What with the restaurant being so busy, we hardly have a moment to spend together at the moment."

"Well, you must do as you please, I'm sure," she sighed again, infusing the phone with a pulsing sense of her disapproval, "of course, your father would not have liked it."

I wanted to sigh now. My father had died more than five years ago, and had he been alive, would not have minded in the slightest that I spend time with my fiancée rather than at home. A modest and humorous man, who always looked on life with a wry and witty eye, he had been a good contrast to the doubt and disbelief my mother was infused with. When he died of cancer, she had nothing left to counteract her darker side. My father would have said that all dreams are able to be accomplished, as long as you work for them. My mother always seemed to think that nothing could be accomplished, so why bother? My sister had taken after my mother, but I, to my relief, had at least tried to take after my father. Without some sort of belief involved, I would never have set up my business, and for that I had my father to thank.

For many years after his death I had done my best to ensure that I went up to see my mother whenever possible, that I spent every holiday with her. I had tried to make up, perhaps, for her losing my dad. But as time went on, perhaps selfishly, perhaps not, I had realised that I needed my own life as well as needing to be there for her. And, again, perhaps selfishly, I found her harder and harder to deal with over the years. People who encase themselves in misery are hard to deal with; they strain on the nerves and on the patience. And even though she was my mother, and I owed her the debt of family and love, I found her hard going at the best of times.

Perhaps that was why I found Billie at once so desirable and so unnerving. Her constant energy and enthusiasm for life was addictive. She was always finding something to be interested in, and cared passionately about politics and the state of the world. She had been raised to believe that she could change things; that she could change the world. My father had thought much like her, but my mother had not. Perhaps, in many ways, Billie was the antidote to my mother that I had never realised I needed so much. Her spirit was like my father's; witty, friendly and always looking for the brighter, lighter side of things. I needed that in my life. When you run a business on your own, you often need to find ways to look on the positive side of things. When I first opened the restaurant, many, including my mother, and my sister Jenny, who took after our mother more than she would care to admit, had believed me to be insane, and had told me so at great length. They had gone over and over the problems and the issues that they believed would stump me in the end, never once telling me that it was a great thing I was doing, despite the risks. But sometimes, we all need to believe that we can do something on the basis of no evidence at all... and I had done it, and was still doing it, despite the disbelief and dire protestations of my living family. I remember returning to our living room a couple of years back from a phone call with my mother where I had been telling her that finally, the restaurant was in profit and I was actually earning a wage, and she had gone into depth with dire prophesises on what might happen next. Billie had taken one look at my face and smiled. She tapped something into the laptop nestled against her on the sofa and turned it to me. It was a little quote, which read:

"*Before you diagnose yourself with depression, or low self-esteem, first make sure that you are not, in fact, just surrounded by assholes.*" William Gibson.

I laughed, and shook my head. "I'm going to tell my mother you called her an asshole," I said.

Billie smiled and turned her laptop back to her. "*Implied*, not called," she said with a shrug and laughed. "I'll tell that that I just showed you a quote, and you identified *her* as the asshole…"

"She doesn't mean to do it," I said, throwing myself onto the couch and making her bounce slightly.

"Then she shouldn't do it," said Billie.

"I know."

"Everything in life takes risk, Henry," she continued, putting one hand into my hair and stroking it softly. It felt heavenly. "And if you risk nothing, you get nothing. The restaurant is doing really well, you should be proud."

"I am."

"Then don't worry about your mum, think about what your dad would have said."

I smiled. "When I first set up the place, he heard my mum going on at me, and said this thing from *Blackadder*," I said.

"Which was?"

"That's the spirit, George," I roared in a rather poor General Melchett impression, "when all else fails, a total pig-headed refusal to look facts in the face will see us through!"

Billie laughed. I often thought how sad it was that she never got to meet my father. The two of them would have got on like pancakes and maple syrup.

I loved my mother and family of course, but at times, I felt so different to them that it was as though I had been placed into the family as a changeling child. Stolen by the fairies and left on the doorstop. If it hadn't have been for my father, I think I would have believed that in truth.

I slowed the car down; the windscreen wipers were creaking furiously as they tried to clear the fluttering snow from my screen, and there was a strange clunking noise in the engine that I had been trying to ignore for some time which was growing ever louder. I was hoping that I was going to make it to the cottage, but the sat-nav in the car had stopped working some miles back as it lost signal, and now I was relying on glancing hastily and nervously at a map laid out on the empty passenger seat with a wind-up torch strategically placed to illuminate it. It wasn't a lot of help. The moor might have had many features which enabled those familiar with it to find their way, but I was a townie, and never more aware of that fact than right now... and according to my calculations, I should have found the village near to the cottage more than an hour ago... I should have been at that warm fire-side with Billie curled up alongside me by now, a glass of wine in hand, and my fingers thinking of working their way along her smooth brown skin and up into her shirt...

Just as I was being distracted by my thoughts of pleasures which I hoped might still await me in the night to come, my eye was caught by something; a flicker, a movement of something white and billowing in the wind, almost straight in front of me. My eyes snapped from the map back to the road, and I slammed on the brakes, causing the car to skid painfully and noisily on the frozen track. I swerved, and just managed to avoid sending the car into one of the carefully positioned ditches at the side of the road, screeching to a halt a few meters from where I had been. As the car stopped, I shifted it to neutral and put my hands to the wheel and leaned my head against them, breathing heavily in shock and panic.

"You're alright," I said, trying to reassure myself by saying the words out loud, "you're alright."

As my beating heart drummed within my chest, I thought... what had I seen? A flash of what looked like a dress or something in the lights of the car... had it been a person, at the side of the road? Had I knocked into someone? The thought made me shiver with fear. Unsteadily, with hands shaking, I opened the door and stepped out into a sharp blast of freezing air. Snow whirled about my head and I shivered, pulling my jacket closer to me. The car had been heated nicely and was lovely and warm. Outside of the car, the wind on the moor was harsh and sharp, biting and snapping at my cheeks and nose. The snow was not the pretty, sweet fall of flakes which graced the front of Christmas cards, but seemed instead to be flung at my face, jumping at my eyes so that I could barely see. The darkness was so complete it was like a vast vacuum, as though I had wandered into outer space. Shining globes of snow blinded me as they whirled about my head. I reached inside the car and grabbed the torch which had fallen to the foot well of the passenger seat, and lifted it up, shining it into the blackness before me.

And then I almost jumped straight out of my skin as the torch lit upon a face, a figure standing on the other side of the car bonnet, staring straight at me. It was the face of a woman, a young woman. Her blonde hair was so fair that it seemed almost paler than the swirling flakes of snow about us, her face pale white, and tinged with blue in the light of the torch, and her eyes... dark, deep black eyes, were regarding me steadily. I made a noise not unlike a surprised sea gull and stumbled backwards, the torch almost slipping from my grasp as I slid into the ditch. At the last moment I managed to regain my footing. With one hand pressed into the cold and sodden bouncy grasses of the moor, I pushed myself upright and whirled the torch around to once more light upon the face of the woman, who had appeared out of nowhere, and was now standing and watching me.

She had not moved from her position on the other side of the car, and appeared to be slightly amused. She looked as though she was trying not to break into a smile, and perhaps I did look as ridiculous as I felt, standing there, panting and squawking, clambering out of the muddy ditch. I felt ridiculous, certainly, and that emotion, combined with the fear she had instilled in me by appearing out of the darkness, made me turn on her in anger.

"Where did you come from?" I demanded, brushing down my coat and staring balefully at her. "You could have had me off the road! You should be walking with a torch, if you are going to be walking here at all, at night!"

She lifted her eyebrows at me slightly, and smiled. Although I felt rather annoyed by the smile, which seemed to indicate a certain kind of dismissal of me as a townie, just another city-boy who couldn't cope with the wilderness of the countryside, I couldn't help but notice that she was quite beautiful. Her long pale hair was tied back, but strands of it were loose and flying in the wind about her face. Her skin was so pale it was almost translucent; she seemed to glow in the light of the car lamps and the light of my torch. Her dark eyes were large and set in a face of delicate features with high cheekbones, which gave her a fragile, child-like, almost elfin quality to her. She was slight of figure, but clearly a young adult, perhaps somewhere between sixteen and twenty, I thought, and dressed in a large black coat, with rather '90s retro combat trousers on, and trainers. Under her coat, barely showing, was a large black hoodie with some sort of yellow circle on it which looked vaguely familiar to me, although I could not place it. I wondered what on earth she was doing out on the moor, in the dark, with no torch and apparently no one with her. Perhaps it was usual for people in the country to wander about in the dark, using the stars to guide them or something, but it wasn't what I was used to. In London, Billie was careful to always have her friends with her if they walked home, and I was insistent on coming to pick her up if she needed me to. I have always believed that a woman should be able to walk wherever she wants, at whatever time she wants, and in an ideal world, that would be the case. But I was also more than aware that there were many dangers from the kind of men who believe that their impulses are more important than another person's choice. I wondered about the parents of this young girl, if she still lived at home, and about her friends, why would they let her wander like this on the moor, alone and at night? Was she lost? She certainly didn't seem perturbed at all, if anything she looked more and more amused.

"Are you going to answer me?" I asked, bristling and feeling more and more like some stuffy old man the more I spoke. What was it about young, self-assured people that could make you feel ancient when you got over thirty? "You shouldn't be out here alone, and in the dark, and with no torch," I said again.

The girl shrugged and pulled her coat about her, as though that was an answer. It infuriated me more.

"Are you on your way home?" I asked, wanting her to say something, anything really, to displace the sense of creeping unease I had about the whole situation.

"I was," she said. Her voice was low, almost husky, as though she had a cold, but without that nasal quality which makes everyone sound like Daffy Duck when it spreads to the nose and throat. I was relieved to hear her answer, even if the answer was short and somewhat evasive. I had been starting to think that I was imagining the whole thing, or that I was going batty.

"You should have a torch," I said again, "I almost hit you back there."

"You didn't swerve because of me." She smiled that irritating smile again, and nodded back along the road. "Look."

I turned and shone the torch along the icy road on which I'd come down only moments before, only to see a long length of sheep's wool attached to a section of fencing. Dancing and fluttering in the wind, it bounced up and down as thought taunting me with its prancing movement. I felt my face flush slightly, despite the cold, and brought the torch back to shine on the girl's face.

"So, you saw me swerve?" I asked slowly, and she nodded at me. "Did you come from a house, then?" I turned the torch to shine ineffectually through the swirling snow and darkness. It lit up nothing, and I could see no lights anywhere which could be from a house.

I looked back at the girl in some confusion, and she smiled at me again. "Come on," she said, "it will be quite a walk" — she looked down at my feet and grimaced slightly — "especially in those shoes."

I looked down at my leather day-shoes, Italian made and rather expensive, they were clearly not made for a trek across the moors. I shook my head at her. "We can go in my car," I protested. "I can take you to your house if you want, you shouldn't stay out here after all, you'll freeze. I'm staying at Trehale Farm Cottage, do you know it?"

She nodded at me. "I know it," she said. "I can take you there."

"Then get in," I felt most relieved and thought happily that I might get to enjoy that glass of wine and the fire after all. What a story to tell Billie that night, and how she would laugh at my ineptitude at anything resembling country life! "Get in and I'll drive you home, as long as you tell me where I'm going first." I smiled at her and she shook her head.

"Your car won't make it," she said, and as though operating on her cue, the car made a rattling noise, not unlike the sound I had been hearing come from the engine for more than an hour. Then it coughed, spluttered, and cut out.

I let out a short cry of despair, and jumped inside. I tried the key over and over, getting the same tired wheezing sound each time, and then looked out of the front window at her. She was still standing in the same place, with that wry, knowing expression on her face. Oddly, she reminded me of my father, although a more striking physical comparison I could not imagine. But there was something of that unfazed and unbeaten attitude to her, a similar kind of amusement, even at seemingly the most dire of times, which seemed to reassure me. I climbed out of the car.

"You can come back and get it in the morning," she said and looked over the moor. As she turned to face the wind, it swept her loose strands of hair backwards, although she hardly even narrowed her eyes to avoid it blinding her. "We'll have to go about Hard Tor."

"We can't trek across the moors in the middle of the night," I said incredulously. "What if we get lost? It could be dangerous."

"It *is* dangerous," she said, nodding and agreeing with me.

"Then shouldn't we do... something else?"

She looked at me, and lifted an eyebrow as though asking, *such as what*? And I felt myself blush slightly. This confident girl was making me feel like a teenager again.

"We could call for help, or if we walk along here, we'd come to a house eventually wouldn't we?" I took my mobile out of my pocket and looked at it despondently; 'No Service'.

She shook her head. "The nearest house is more than four miles, along the road," she said, "you've come a long way out of your way tonight. It will be quicker to cut across. I know the way."

I frowned at her, could that be right? Four miles? It seemed incredible, and yet, she seemed to know where she was and what she was doing. It didn't seem as though I had much choice but to go with her and hope that this strange girl did know as much as she said she did.

"I'll get my bag," I said, starting to reach into the back for it, but she stopped me.

"Come as you are," she said and her words seemed to strike some memory within me… something I'd not heard for a long time. "You can come back for your things in the morning. For now, you shouldn't burden yourself."

I pulled a face, but agreed that she was right. I did, however, pull off my shoes and replaced them with the new hiking boots I'd bought for this trip. Locking the car, and buttoning my long coat around me, and covering that one with a waterproof, I grasped the torch in my hands, and nodded to her. "Alright then, let's go," I said.

She nodded at me and lifted a hand, pointing at into the darkness. "We go this way," she said. "Keep up and be careful of your feet. Shine the torch to light the ground, or you could stumble, the ground is uneven."

"But, how will you see, if I don't shine the torch outwards?"

"I don't need the torch to see," she smiled, and I had to agree that since she had managed to come to my aid without the benefit of a torch or light, she must be right. Perhaps she was used to walking at night.

"Alright," I said, and started onto the bouncy, ice-covered grasses of the moor at her heels. "I haven't thanked you," I said.

"No, you haven't." I could hear the same touch of amusement in her voice as she spoke and it made me smile, even through my huffing and puffing as we walked. Although the restaurant kept me busy, it wasn't quite the same as taking regular exercise. I had been meaning to take up jogging for some time, and never got around to it. But as the ice of the air bit into my lungs, and as I felt the soft folds about my middle start to dance a little with the walking, I vowed to take up jogging this New Year. I felt quite ancient and flabsome next to the lithe little creature before me who seemed to drift and glide over the moors with ease.

"Well, thank you," I said. "How did you come to be passing by here at this time anyway? You said there are no houses nearby, you can't have been wandering the moors for pleasure at this time and in this weather?"

"You should save your breath and watch your footing," she said, and once more on cue with her words, I stumbled a little. "Exhausting yourself on the moors can be dangerous."

"You live nearby then?"

"I did."

A strange choice of tense, I thought, and then thought that it was Christmas, so she must mean she was home visiting. "You are home from uni then?" I asked.

"I never went."

"Well, there's time for that later, if you want to go," I said. "I took a year out myself…"

She stopped and turned to me. I stumbled to a halt and my torch lit up her dark eyes. She did not blink, but fixed me with a stare that was so different to the other looks she had given me that it quite chilled my bones. She stared steadily, but with anger in her eyes. Her cheeks were pinched and her skin looked rather blue in the cold and the light of my torch. "The moor *is* dangerous," she said softly, calmly, but with an edge of warning to it so severe I felt as though I was a child being told off by a parent. "Pay attention to what you are doing, and follow me."

I nodded dumbly at her, not wanting to make the slight girl angry with me. Fear coursed through my blood, but of what exactly, I hardly knew. It was not as though the girl was of any physical threat to me; she was tiny, and I was not a small man, I stood head and shoulders over many… but yet, there was in her voice and in her manner such a measure of control and sternness that I was unnerved. I lapsed into silence as I followed her.

Soon enough, I was glad of the silence. It was a hard trudge across the moor. The grass was bouncy, hard and covered in the still-falling snow, and it was often deceptive. More than once my foot went down onto seemingly solid grass only to plunge through a thin sheet of ice and into a pool of murky water. The mounds and bumps across the land were hard to navigate, and although I had little way of finding where we were or where we were heading, I was sure we must be going uphill, because I was rapidly becoming exhausted. My coat was damp under the waterproof with sweat, but as I moved to take off a layer the girl turned and shook her head at me.

"Keep it on," she advised sharply. "You'll need it as we reach the top of Hard Tor, it doesn't do to get cold out here."

Seeing as she looked as much like a frozen woman as anything else, with her pale, almost blue skin, I felt she should have little to say on the matter, but I took her advice and kept it on. As we climbed the steep side of the Tor, wending out way about it, rather than going straight over, the wind picked up mightily, roaring about me and picking its way through every part of my clothing. Despite my layers of clothing, the thick coat and good waterproof I had, I could feel the icy winter chill through every part of me. The girl had been right again, I needed every layer I had against the cold out here. I started to shiver, but my skin felt hot to the touch, as though I had a fever.

The bouncing light of the torch picked up crops of stones and ferns, gorse here and there bristling and bobbing in the wind. The snow fell straight in front of my eyes, blinding me, but all the time, as I lumbered and stumbled through the land, the girl walked on just ahead of me with a lightness and grace which I could never have matched. She picked her way through the gorse and fern, along small paths which I could barely see through the grey rocks, looking as though she was wandering on a bright sunny morning, without a care in the world.

We walked this way for perhaps an hour, with me stumbling behind her. I grew colder and colder, despite the warmth pumped forth from my blood with the exercise. My nose felt as though it was not there anymore, and my cheeks were raw with the onslaught of the wind and the snow. My feet and hands were growing numb in the cold, and my mind was starting to wander. I felt as though I was faltering and stumbling through a dream… as though none of this was really real, as though I had fallen asleep in the car when it had broken down and I had dreamed all of this… I started to think that that might be the case, but then, the car had broken down *after* the girl appeared, hadn't it? Or had it? I could not seem to remember. My thoughts were jumbled and confused. I started to feel quite sick, and hot… I was hot for some reason… I needed to take off this coat, I thought, fumbling for the buttons.

And then her face was right in front of me again, and I jumped backwards. My heart boomed inside my ears with sudden fright and I stared at her.

"Don't do that," she warned, her voice stern but kind, "your mind is confused. It is the cold, it does that to you… keep your coat on, and follow me, it's not far now." She smiled at me. "Billie is waiting for you," she whispered. I stared at her as she turned towards the unseen path which only she could determine once more. "There is a warm fire ready for you at the cottage… she's worried… you need to get back to her."

I opened my mouth to ask her how she knew about Billie, but I could barely gather the strength to speak. I felt numb all over, confused, heavy. I wanted nothing more than to lie down on the springy grass with my head against a cool rock and fall asleep. But something in her words seemed to reach through to me, and although I did not want to, although all I wanted to do was lie down, I lurched after her again, walking like a drunken man staggering home on a Friday night.

We started to walk downwards; the path became easier, the wind lessened. Although the snow still fell and whipped about me in little clouds, I started to be able to see once more, my eyes no longer blinded by the howling wind. I could see lights, distant they seemed in the haze of the snow, but they were there.

"Billie is waiting," the girl called; her voice almost sing-song, like a lullaby. I staggered after her, feeling like a child being led on a merry dance.

At a stone wall, where the open moor met the garden of a small cottage, she stopped and turned to me. I lifted the torch wearily, hardly getting the light off the ground. I was panting heavily, and felt more tired than I had ever been. My thoughts swam in the soup of my mind, falling over each other, becoming befuddled. I looked at the lights of the cottage, spilling out over the dark moor with cheerful abandon with confused eyes. And then I looked back at the girl.

"Go inside, Henry," she said softly, smiling at me with that wry smile. "Go inside and get warm. All will be well now."

"When did I tell you my name?" I muttered dully, lifting the torch to shine on her face better.

"I always know," she whispered, her voice becoming drowned by the noise of the wind, "I always… just know."

The torch light shone on her; that pale skin, that blonde hair, that wry smile. She looked so pretty, like a little white and blonde fairy standing in the snow. She smiled at me again, and I felt the corners of my frozen mouth smile back at her, mirroring the expression on her face. For a moment, we just stood there, bathed in the flickering lights of the cottage and the bright glare of the torch… And then, suddenly, she vanished.

I stared at the space where she had stood for a moment, paralysed with shock, then I threw the torch light about, thinking that she had fallen, calling out for her, even though I didn't know her name. "Where are you?" I shouted, all my dazed confusion seeming to lift for a moment as I panicked. "Where have you gone?" The torch beam hit the grasses on the moor, shone over the silver-grey rocks which peppered the earth beneath my feet. The snow reflected the light back at me, blinding my red-raw eyes and making them swim with tears. "Where are you?" I screamed into the darkness.

And then from the cottage, there was another voice, one so familiar that the sound of it hurt my heart to hear it. I was so relieved. "Henry?" Billie called, standing hesitantly at the door, the glowing light of the cottage at her back lighting her up as though her shadow was on fire. "Henry, is that you? Where have you been? I've been worried sick!"

"Billie!" I shouted, my voice coming from me in a high-pitched squeal. "Billie! You have to help me! Come quickly!"

She pulled on a coat and came racing to me, a large flashlight in her hands. When she saw the state of me, dishevelled, wet, covered in mud and snow, she seemed to blanche slightly and then tried to drag me indoors. "Where's your car? Did you *walk* here? What happened to you? You need to get indoors, now!"

"I can't, I can't! There was a girl here, Billie, a girl! My car, it broke down. She helped me, guided me across the moor. I was lost, but she found me."

"A girl?" she asked, looking around her and shining her torch, "what girl?" She looked at me worriedly and put a hand to my cheek. "You're *frozen*, Henry," she said, "we need to get you indoors."

"There was a *girl*, Billie," I shouted at her, knowing I was making no sense at all, "she was here one minute and gone the next..." I turned this way and that, flashing my torch about me. "I tell you, she was *here*. Please, Billie, maybe she fell and she's hurt."

Billie indulged me for more than half an hour as we searched and searched the area about the house for signs of the strange girl who had come to my rescue on the moor, but there was nothing. Billie even went and got her car, shining the headlamps over the moor, and there was still nothing. As we searched and found nothing, over and over again, I saw Billie looking at me in concern, obviously believing that I had imagined all of this, and was delirious. In all honestly, I was no longer sure myself. Had I imagined it all?

In the fright and panic at the girl suddenly vanishing, I seemed to have lost the dull confusion of my mind. I was a sharp spike of thought and action, looking here there and everywhere to find the girl. But she was no-where to be seen. Eventually, I let

Billie take me in the house, but even as she stripped me of my wet clothes and wrapped me up in warm, dry clothes as I shivered by the fire, I made her call the police station. I told her the story of my crash, and my saviour, and although I knew she wondered if I had imagined it all, she still listened and agreed to call the police station.

"Even if she's not in trouble at the moment, she shouldn't be out on the moors now, it's dangerous," I said through my rattling teeth.

"If what you've said is all true, Henry, then if that girl is out there then she knows just what she's doing… better than you did, anyway," said Billie, but agreed to call. She also called the doctor, without asking me, using a sheet of local telephone numbers left by the cottage owners for emergencies. She came back in looking perturbed, and a little angry.

"What is it?" I asked, my teeth still chattering as I sat close to the fire. Dry clothes and a warm blanket were wrapped about me, but the fire seemed to reach no part of my skin or flesh. I felt as though I might never get warm again.

"The police, sort of, *laughed* at me," she replied in an angry tone. "They said that it was a full four months until April Fool's and I ought not to waste their time." She shook her head, looking puzzled and annoyed. "But the doctor *is* coming," she said.

"Coming out here, on Christmas Eve?"

"He lives right near-by, apparently, and he wanted to check you over for himself," she nodded curtly, with approval, "at least there's *someone* in this part of the world doing their job." She sat down next to me, got under the blanket and pulled me to her. What the fire and the blanket failed to do, Billie, it seemed, could. Slowly, and rather painfully, I felt her body heat warming me. I felt sleepy and confused, and still worried about that girl out there in the snow and the wind.

"I was worried about you," she said with a slight reproving note to her voice.

"I didn't mean for my car to break down."

"I know that, of course, I just wanted you to know..." she tailed off as we saw the lights of a car coming up the road. "That was quick," she said as she went to open the door.

The doctor was called Gerry Eastland, and insisted on calling me Mr Anderson all the way through his examination of me; calling Billie Ms Green. He was about seventy years of age, with a full head of white hair and a little portly lump around the middle, but pretty spry for his age. I wondered why he hadn't retired, but he seemed to be in fine health, and given the care he seemed to give to his job, I figured he was one of those people, like me, who really loved what they did.

It was Billie who asked him about the strange attitude of the police, and when he heard the story, his face went a little grey, and then he flushed, as though embarrassed. He sat down on the edge of the little sofa and stared at me. "Sounds like you had a lucky escape there, Mr Anderson," he said. "A night like this, and out on the moors... Bodmin's not as big as some moors, but it's easy to get lost, and with the elements as they were, you could have been in danger."

"That's what she kept saying," I nodded. "The girl who found me; she kept saying that the moors were dangerous."

Gerry nodded slowly, and narrowed his eyes at me. "You've never been to these parts before?" he asked abruptly.

I shook my head. "We came down to Looe when I was a kid," I said, "but not up here, I don't think, why?"

"Then you've heard no stories locally... when you were coming up here?"

"I only stopped once, at a petrol station in Plymouth," I said, "and I didn't ask them anything about the moors… why?"

He sighed a little and smiled awkwardly at Billie and me. "The girl that you saw Mr Anderson… blonde hair, dark eyes… wearing a dark coat and a Nirvana top?"

"Yes…" I said slowly, feeling my heart jump into my chest, and suddenly realizing where I had seen that yellow circle logo before, "you know her then?"

He shook his head a little. "No," he said. "I *knew* her."

I noted the change in tense and felt as though all the snow and ice of the moors had rushed inside me. I shivered, although not because of the cold this time. There was something in his expression which chilled me. "What do you mean?" I asked.

He smiled that awkward smile once again and glanced at Billie who was biting her lip and staring at the doctor with concern in her face. "Mr Anderson… what I'm about to say to you will no doubt convince you that I've been at the Christmas brandy," he said and smiled without humour, "or that us country folk out here on the moors have all gone *Bodmin* as the expression goes… but there is a reason the police station didn't believe you, Ms Green." Gerry spread his hands, "and I'm not sure I'd believe it myself… if it wasn't for all the stories over the years."

"What stories?" I asked, sitting up and throwing the blanket back, "what do you mean?"

"I think that the girl you met tonight, Mr Anderson, was called Lucy Hicks. And there's no need to go looking for her on the moors… you see, Lucy Hicks is what you might call our resident ghost."

I stared at him in disbelief. "You cannot be serious," I said, almost laughing. "I don't believe in ghosts."

He shrugged. "Many a person who has met her has said the same thing," he said, "but seen her they have, and the fact is, Mr Anderson, that Lucy Hicks died in the winter of 1992." He looked at me and pursed his lips together. "Her family moved down here from London, just another family, looking to live the good life and escape the town… you know how it goes. They had a small-holding not far from here. Not long after they came down, her parents split up, and Lucy was left with her mother." He shook his head. "Plenty of us knew there was something wrong there," he said with a sense of grief and guilt in his voice, "but back then… it wasn't *done*, as it is now, to try to interfere, and no one seemed to know for sure, but it seemed that Mrs Hicks was not a well woman, was… abusive to her daughter. One night in that winter they had a big fight. Lucy went out, for a walk her mother said, and never came back. Her mother didn't call the police for several days; said that she thought Lucy had gone to friends, but all of us wondered."

He looked me in the eyes for the first time in his story; his eyes were sad, and strained. "We found her body five days later, Mr Anderson, near to Hard Tor. It looked as though she had slipped and hit her head, but I always wondered about it. The police investigated, took Lucy's mother in for questioning, but there was no evidence on the scene to prove that it had been anything other than an accident, and we never found out in truth if Lucy slipped and fell, and then died of exposure, or…" he tailed off, and I continued,

"Or if her mother pushed her?" I finished. He nodded, his face a little grey.

"The mother moved out of the area after that. And that was when the stories started… usually it was from walkers; hikers out on the moor who had lost the way they were going, said that a nice young lady, who obviously knew her way around, had come as if from nowhere and told them the way to go… sometimes it was people like you, in real trouble, cars broken down, or got a flat and didn't have a spare… said they met a young girl with pale hair and dark eyes who popped up and took them where they needed to go, or to the village where they could get help." He smiled at me again. "Believe what you wish to believe, Mr Anderson," he shrugged. "But the reason the police laughed at Ms Green here is because they have heard that story a hundred times, and they know that there is no *living* girl out wandering the moor, not anymore…"

He looked about him and clapped his hands on his thighs, getting up.

"Wait a moment," I said. "You can't just tell me something like that and then go! What am I supposed to do with that?"

"Do… whatever you like with it, Mr Anderson. I can only tell you what I know." He smiled at me, "perhaps you imagined the whole thing, eh? Perhaps it was a figment of your imagination."

"That's a very big figment to come to terms with," I said. "I don't believe in ghosts." The last remark was said almost petulantly, as though I'd been told I couldn't have more pudding by my mother.

"Then you'll better put it down to the close shave you had with hypothermia." He nodded to Billie. "You have my number, check on him through the night, but I think we're in the clear. I'll come and see you tomorrow."

"That's very kind of you, Doctor, thank you," she said, taking him to the door.

When she came back, she was biting her lip again and staring at me.

"Do you think I imagined all that?" I asked.

"Do you?"

"No."

"Then I believe that what you saw was real, Henry," she said, coming closer to me and pulling me to her. "And whatever happened, and however you got here… I'm just glad that you did get here. And if something, or someone helped you get here, then I'm grateful to them, more grateful than I'll ever be able to say."

I put my head against her breast and nodded. "Me too," I whispered.

*

Two days later, after a lot more conversation with the reluctantly informative doctor, and an internet search, saw me standing in the memorial gardens of a local church, staring at a small brass plaque. It read:

In memory of Lucy Audrey Hicks
Beloved Daughter
1975 - 1992

"It's so small," I said in a low voice to Billie who stood at my side holding my hand. "Doesn't it seem small?"

She nodded and squeezed my hand. I looked around, feeling a little foolish. "I don't know what to say," I said.

"Just say what comes to you, Henry," whispered Billie.

I looked at the plaque again. "Thank you," I said simply. "Thank you for helping me out, Lucy." I reached down and placed the bunch of flowers we had bought in the village against the wall under her plaque. "Thank you for saving me."

We stood there for a while, staring at the plaque on the wall in that little garden, and then we turned and walked back to our car, heading back to London, to a life which I somehow felt had been saved for me, by the strange, wry girl I had met on the moor.

Hot Toddy

Mary waited until they were all asleep.

It could be hard, when the house was so full of people on Christmas night, to keep her appointment, but, bedevilled by food and exhausted by the constant demands of the grandchildren, her two sons and their respective wives had headed for bed relatively early this Christmas. Mary lay in her bed with the covers pulled up to her neck, and waited for the house to quiet down to the feeling of peace which meant slumber had reached all inhabitants. Then she pulled back the covers, and moved breathlessly to the door.

She opened it a crack, and listened. She could hear nothing from the attic rooms above where her eldest son, Jack, and his wife and ten-year-old son, Albert, were. Jack and Hilde were staying in the attic rooms where once, as children, her two sons had slept and done their homework, or played in the spare room at the end. Mary and her husband had had their sons later in life; for some reason children did not come to them until they were in their late thirties and early forties, but she had never regretted being older than many of her friends to have her children. She was just glad they had come eventually. Mary listened quietly. She could hear nothing from above, and nothing from the guest bedroom which her youngest son, Michael, and his wife had claimed for this Christmas visit with their six-year-old, Sarah. She listened for another moment, and then she crept from her room, and started for the stairs.

Mary slunk along the hallway of the three-storied Victorian end-terrace house which she had lived in since her marriage, many, many years ago. On the landing, the old grandfather clock clicked as it approached midnight. Mary crept down the hallway and reached the stairs; she paused to listen again, but could hear nothing other than the sonorous half-snores of Jack from above. She smiled. His father had snored too; it seemed some things were forever to be carried on in the family bloodline. She reached the stairs and for a moment, cursed the aches in her hips and the creaking of her bones. When she was a young woman she had never thought about all the little aches and pains which came with age, and now that she was nearing eighty, she couldn't imagine a time when all these little passengers in her body did not make their presence felt. The chill of the night pervaded through the old house and touched on her little pains, making them worse. It would have been easier to go back to the warmth of her bed, but this was a yearly appointment which she longed for, and loved to keep. Ever since the first time it had occurred…

Hardly daring to breathe, Mary reached the bottom of the stairs and listened again for any sign that she had disrupted the sleep of her sons or their families, but she could hear nothing. She made her way into the kitchen and took up a little pan, pouring water into it from a jug she had prepared earlier, so that the household would not hear her running water from the tap in the night. She checked her watch; she still had a few minutes before the appointment. As the water boiled on the electric stove, she poured a measure of good single-malt whisky into a cup, and mixed in a spoonful of thick, golden honey. Then she took cloves from her herb rack, and added two to the cup of whisky and honey. The water boiled, and she took it off the heat as she poured a dash of lemon juice into the cup and added a thin slice of lemon as well, so thinly sliced that its flesh was almost transparent in the moonlight. When the water had cooled a little, she topped up the cup to half-way with it and inhaled the sweet, rich, spiced smell which wafted from the cup in plumes of ghostly steam, and took it into the living room.

She sat down in her chair, and set the hot toddy next to the seat of the empty chair at her side. As she looked at the little cup, set on its placemat, she felt the old ache come to her heart. An old pain pervaded her heart, much more familiar and still more tender than all the aches which had made their home in her joints and through her body. She smiled a little, sadly, as she looked at the cup and felt her old, familiar ache. There was nothing that could compare to the pain of loss. It was more powerful than any hurt the body could produce. But now the pain was like an old friend, for she knew it so well. It did not hurt her so much now, when it came to her. It was like an echo that constantly sounded in her heart. She merely accepted the feeling, and carried it with her each day. But tonight, it came with a sense of happiness too, for soon enough *he* would be coming back…

She looked at her watch again as the hot toddy cooled, puffing out little wisps of steam which travelled on the cold night air. This house was full of draughts and cracks and crannies. The grandchildren loved to play hide and seek here, whenever they came for Christmas, for there were so many places to hide. Her son, Jack, had been saying that he would get a man around to help her with all the little DIY jobs which needed doing, but Mary was used to the chill of the house, the draughts, and the little noises it made. The house had been her constant companion all these years that she had lived here with her husband and family, and then when she had lived here alone. Without the little draughts and creaks, it wouldn't feel so much like home to her… wouldn't be the same creature. And she knew that Jack would not remember to send any such man; it wasn't because he didn't care, it was just that he was so busy in his own life that such things went out of his head as soon as he returned home. She didn't mind, she thought, smiling. It was nice to know that her sons worried for her, and even nicer that many times they forgot to carry out the things they promised. She didn't want them to send tradesmen around to fix things she didn't want fixing. But whenever they suggested anything, she would nod and smile because she knew it reassured them. Sometimes, with children, it is best to nod and smile along, no matter how old they were…

She looked at her watch and *tsked* slightly.

"Am I being told off already?" asked a low, soft voice at her side.

Mary closed her eyes with pleasure and smiled. She nodded her head a little and let out a quiet laugh. "Aren't you always? You should be used to it by now." She turned her head and opened her eyes to look into the warm brown eyes of the man she had loved for more than sixty years. He was sitting in his chair at her side, his shock of grey hair thick upon his head. Most men lost their hair when they grew old, but not Albe. His friends had given him the nick-name of Einstein, not for a remarkable brain, but for his remarkable hair… His handsome face was crinkled and lined, like a fallen crab-apple, but she could still see the bold jaw and strong cheekbones of the man she had fallen in love with when they were just young things. He was grinning at her, his face now no longer creased and darkened by the pain of his last days; he looked at her with merry eyes and leaned over to kiss her.

She could not feel the kiss on her cheek, but she blushed a little all the same. It was the magic of Albe; that he could always make her feel like a girl, even when she was now a girl caught in the body of an old woman. She didn't need to feel the touch of his lips on her cheek, she could imagine it, and that was enough.

Albe looked around and nodded at the windows. "You changed the curtains?"

"Hilde did," she said, a little ruefully.

Albe laughed softly. "If you don't like them, Mary, then why let her do it?"

Mary breathed in through her nose and sighed the air out the same way. "It made Jack happy for Hilde to help me out with some redecorating," she said with a shrug, "and I can live with them."

"Still worried about you, are they?"

She shrugged. "They just like to show they care, what's wrong with that?"

"Depends..." he smiled at her again. "On how hideous the curtains they choose are."

She laughed a little and nodded to the cup at his side. "Well?" she asked. "Did I make it right this year?"

Albe assumed a look of sanctimonious concentration as he leaned over the armrest of his chair and took a deep sniff at the cup. He sat back and seemed to ponder his response until she let out a little grunt of annoyance at his delay. He turned and nodded to her with approval. "The right mixture of honey and whisky, good draught of lemon... and not too much water, unlike last year..."

"Jack surprised me in the kitchen making the damn thing last year!" Mary laughed, a little too loudly. They simultaneously made shushing motions at each other and then grinned like teenagers doing something naughty. "He made me jump and I slopped too much water in!" she whispered. "It was all I could do to get rid of him before you appeared... he thought I was going round the ruddy bend, of course... still does, I think."

"Ah, worried about your sanity now, are they?"

Mary shrugged. "I think they're more worried I'll fall down the stairs and break a hip, or take a tumble when I go to the market." She held out her arm and showed him some mottled bruises on her skin. "Any time I bump into anything now I get marked as though I've been in a pub brawl," she sighed, and rubbed at her arm. "I used to have such pretty skin."

"You still do, my love," Albe said gamely and sat back, looking at her.

"What?" she asked.

"You are more beautiful now than when I first met you, you know?" he said, almost shyly.

"With all the wrinkles and the crinkles?" she laughed but felt her cheeks heat a little as his words brushed over them. "I'm getting old, now, Albe."

"A beautiful woman is a beautiful woman, no matter her age," he said earnestly. "Age doesn't negate beauty, it only changes it, softens it… youth has no more claim on beauty than it does on wisdom. It's only adverts that make you think it does. And of course they want you to think that beauty has to be *made* and *created* and age has to be stalled and stopped in every way… they want to sell their potions and lotions, don't they?"

"Don't start on that again, dear."

"Well, it ridiculous isn't it… telling women they are worth a bottle of shampoo… no wonder so many young girls have issues with their bodies… as if any person is so worthless that they could be held to be the same value as some soap for the hair…"

She shook her head, and waited for him to stop. Eventually, he noted her silence and turned to her. She shook her head at him and he laughed. "Was I going on again?"

"Always, dear."

He smiled and sighed. "Tell me about the boys then," he said. "Anything new?"

"Michael and Rebecca are going to have another child."

"Really?" Albe looked quite pleased. "Another sprog in the family. Good genes, you see? Have they thought of a name yet?"

Mary laughed. "They aren't even aware they are having one, yet."

"What do you mean?"

"Oh, I could tell the moment she arrived yesterday, Albe. But I don't think she's cottoned on yet. Perhaps no more than a month I'd guess."

"Aren't you going to tell them?"

"And spoil all the fun for them? Albert Richard Gardiner, you know I'd never do any such thing! Finding out you're going to have a child is something that should be shared between a couple privately first. I wouldn't dream of spoiling all the intimate little secrecies this will cause between them. They'll tell me when they know, and when they want others to know."

"And you'll act suitably surprised." He shook his head. "You always had a devious mind, my dear."

"Well then it was well suited to the man I married, wasn't it?" she smiled at him.

"And how is Jack?"

"Busy, busy, busy, as per usual," she sighed. "He tries to do too much, takes on too many things. I worry about him at times. Seems like he might run out of steam one morning... but then Hilde is the same way... and little Albe seems to be walking in their footsteps. He has more after-school activities than I know how he has time to do them... but they all seem happy, if generally exhausted."

"Well, it's good for kids to try lots of things when they are young," said Albe thoughtfully, "makes them able to find what they do like, and pursue it… does Albe still want to be an astronaut?"

Mary shook her head. "A chiropodist," she said dryly.

"What? Why?"

She shook her head. "I don't know really… apparently someone told him that they make a lot of money, and he thought that might be good. He told me he doesn't mind feet, so he thought it might be a good job to have… and then he could make hobby race cars when he wasn't at work."

Albe shook his head. "Money doesn't make anyone happy," he said gravely. "Just look at the people who have lots of money, all barmy…" He looked over at her. "Try to encourage him to do another job, won't you?"

She smiled and patted the arm of his chair. "It won't last, dear. Remember all the things that you thought you'd be? And if it does, then why worry? At least it's an achievable goal. There are worse jobs."

Albe looked none too convinced. "What about Sarah?" he asked, speaking of Michael and Rebecca's girl.

Mary smiled. "A little tyrant, but a charming one. She commands that house, and any other she comes into. She'll be a force to be reckoned with when she's a teenager, I tell you."

Albe grunted a laugh and shook his head. "I never worry about that one," he said a little wistfully, "I just wish I had had a chance to hold her when she was a baby."

"I know, dear." Mary's eyes filled with tears a little as she thought of that first Christmas when Albe hadn't been with the family. When Sarah had been born in the middle of the January that followed, and their car had almost broken down in a snow drift on the way to hospital. It had been a confused and calamitous manner of entering the world, but all the family had made it to the hospital to stand around Rebecca's bed and coo at the new arrival, feeling both sad and happy that this new person was here, and that their Albe was gone.

"And then the next Christmas... you appeared here for the first time," Mary said, carrying on her thoughts as though Albert could hear them. "Gave me a funny turn, you did. Thought I might have a heart attack and join you when you appeared at my side in the dark!"

"I smelt the hot toddy you made." He looked at her with warm eyes. "And I knew you were missing me. You never drink those things yourself, so why make one then? You made it to remember me, because I always drank a hot toddy at Christmas, and you looked so very lonesome in your big chair."

"It would be nice if you could come more than once a year," she reprimanded, wiping away a little tear at the corner of her eyes.

"I wish I could too," he said, "but for some reason..."

"Well, it was the night you died, of course." Mary shook her head. "Couldn't have chosen another night, could you? Supposed to be the happiest day of the year..."

"I *really* didn't have a choice, dear," Albe said stiffly.

A noise on the stairs made them both stop. Mary looked over and shook her head at her husband. Gradually, he faded into nothingness. She breathed a sigh of relief as she heard footsteps coming down the stairs and into the room. It was her youngest son, Michael, a grown man now of thirty-eight, who started when he saw her sitting in the dark with the cooling cup of whisky at her side.

"Mum? What are you doing?"

She smiled at him and picked up the cup. "Couldn't sleep, dear, just came down for a night cap. Did you want something?"

"I… just came down for some water," he said, looking at her anxiously. "Are you sure you're alright, Mum? It's a bit odd, sitting here in the dark…"

"If I put the light on, it will just wake me up more." She smiled at him, seeing the lines of worry move over his face. He looked like he did when he was a boy, trying to find the solution to a homework problem. "I'm fine, dear. You take your water back up to bed."

"You shouldn't walk up the stairs in the dark, Mum," he warned, walking to the kitchen and pouring a glass of water. "You could trip over."

"I know those stairs as well as I know you, Michael James Gardiner," she said. "And I shan't trip, I promise you. Now, go back up to bed."

Michael paused at the door, taking a sip of water. "Is it Dad?" he asked softly. "Were you thinking about him?"

Mary smiled at her son. "In many ways, more so than you can ever imagine, Michael, I am always thinking about your father. But not in a bad way, or a sorry way… I still talk to him sometimes, when I'm alone, and I know just what he'd say to advise me… that's what comes of knowing someone that long, I suppose." She smiled at her son and shook her head. "You go back to bed. I'm fine."

He walked over and kissed the top of her grey hair. "I love you," he said gruffly, and then added, "just be careful on those stairs, won't you?"

"I will take each step one at a time, rather than three at a time as I used to," she grinned and shooed him away. "Go back to Rebecca, she might wake and wonder where you are."

Michael nodded, and took his water back up the stairs. As her son disappeared, Albe took shape once more at her side.

"That was close," he said with an impish grin. "Felt a bit like that time I snuck into your room when we were courting, and your dad almost found me there!"

Mary laughed. "I never saw someone climb out of a window so fast… I was sure you'd fallen."

"I did… Luckily for me, your dad's rose bushes got in the way," he said with a grimace, "although I'm not sure it was worth it for all the thorns I had to remove from my rear."

"I wasn't worth a few thorns? Well, I wish I'd known that!" she smiled at him as he leaned over to her.

"I take it back," he whispered. "You were worth every thorn I had to pull out of my rear… and you'd be worth a thousand more…"

"Worth a thousand thorns," she smiled, putting her lips to his even though she felt nothing but the air. "So much better than worth a bottle of shampoo."

He sighed. "My time is ending once more," he said.

Mary nodded to him. "I know," she said in a little voice.

"I will see you next year, my love?"

"Unless I do take a fall as Michael seems sure I will, and come to you faster than that."

Albe shook his head. "They need you, Mary. Stay with them a while longer."

"I miss you," she said, her voice breaking.

"I miss you too… but you know that one day, we will have all the time we could ever want together."

"I am quite looking forward to it."

He smiled and nodded. "Until next year, my love."

"Until next year."

"I love you."

Mary smiled. "I love you too, Albe…"

She watched as the figure of her husband disappeared slowly, his arms and legs fading against the brown leather covers of the chair; his brown eyes twinkling in the darkness as they dissipated. The shock of grey hair on his head waned into wisps of smoke which wafted through the air. She sat there for a moment, looking at his chair as the old familiar pain of loss came back to her heart, and she nodded to feel it within her… almost like a feeling of homesickness, a feeling of longing for something which was now gone.

"I miss you… every day that you aren't here, I miss you," she said to the nothingness. She felt keen, bright tears come to her eyes once more, and let them come, let them roll down her cheeks. And then she stood and took the cup into the kitchen and stood at the window. She took a sip of the cold toddy in her hands and made a face. However right the mixture was, it was not her drink. But the taste of it on her lips reminded her of Albe, and of many Christmases where they had laughed and eaten together. When they had opened presents and some where they had argued. But they had always been together, almost all of their lives had been spent together, just as she knew that one day, when the time came, they would spend their deaths together too.

She set down the cup, and went back up to bed. She didn't turn on the light, as she had promised she would do to her son; she had no need to. Her feet might be getting old, but she was as sure of her steps now as she had been when she was young. Mary climbed into bed with a little sigh of relief. It was good to feel the warm covers about her once more. She put her head down and fell into a deep sleep, where she dreamed about the days when she and Albe were young, and he had risked the anger of her father, by appearing at her window in the middle of the night to steal a kiss from her…

As she slept, there was a little smile on her face, and in the darkness, a pale hand reached out to cup her face with its palm. Albe smiled at the face of his sleeping wife. And, making sure that she was safe back in bed, he walked unseen and silent through the rooms of his old house, to take one last look at his children and grandchildren, before the dawn came and his time amongst the living was done.

Christmas was a time to visit with the family, after all, Albe thought, as he moved silently through the rooms of his house.

Roger Reed and the Road Kill Rabbit

Rodger Reed was a busy man; he was busy all the time and made sure people knew it. His job was important, far more important than anyone else', he was sure, and he had little time for the courtesies of life, unless, of course, those courtesies were to be paid to someone who was higher up than him, or more wealthy than him. Then, he had all the time in the world.

It was because Rodger was so very busy that he drove so very fast. Whether in the city where he worked as head manager of several branches, or whether, like now, when he was driving home to see his parents for the Christmas break, he always tried to drive at the very top speed that he could accomplish, bombing down the country lanes towards the old pile which his father had bought with his retirement funds and a lifetime of work as an investment banker in the city.

Rodger hadn't really wanted to go home for Christmas, but his father had told him that there was an important issue that needed to be discussed, and Rodger believed that this would be the old man's will. As the eldest of three children, Rodger already believed that he would take the lion's share of the inheritance when the old man finally popped his clogs. His parents were conservative down to their boots, and believed in the age-old tradition of leaving their estate, which consisted of a country pile, lots of land and a huge volume of cash, to their eldest son, to continue the legacy they had started. Rodger believed that he of all their three children would gain the most out of their deaths, but of course, sometimes such things needed a little push in the right direction. He did not want his younger brother and sister getting their greedy hands on *his* money, and so the fancy parties he would have attended in London had to be missed this year; he had to make an appearance at his family home.

It was as Rodger was pondering with some relish on the fat inheritance which would one day come his way, and how he would eventually sell off the ghastly Tudor mansion his parents had bought, and the land, for a tidy sum, when he whizzed around a corner on one of the small country lanes. Straight in front of him, its ears raised and a curious expression of shock on its face was a small brown rabbit with a cotton-bob tail. Without attempting to slow down, Rodger ploughed straight into the rabbit with the front of his BMW, causing the tiny creature to spin sickeningly, sending its corpse flying out of the side of the underbelly of his car. The body of the mangled dead rabbit flew across the road and fell against the hedge; a bleeding, prostrate pile of fur and flesh.

Rodger did not think twice about killing the rabbit. To him it was just another thing in his way. Pushing his foot down once more, he zoomed off through the lanes, forcing another driver to almost crash into a hedge, trying to avoid him on another bend. Rodger grinned to see the driver of the other car doing a 'wanker' sign at him in his rear mirror as he flew off down the lane; Rodger rather liked seeing that people didn't like him very much, especially when they couldn't do anything about it; it made him feel powerful.

As Rodger glanced in his rear mirror at the driver of the other car, something caught the corner of his eye. He did a double take, and even slowed down a little... for a moment it had looked as though there was something in the back of the car... something small, something brown... he twisted his neck and looked behind him, but there was nothing. Rodger shrugged and pressed his accelerator down once more; he wanted to get to the family pile before dark, and have a large whisky, the best his father could afford, and the old man could afford the very best.

Rodger's car pulled up in front of the Tudor mansion, sending waves of tiny white ornamental pebbles flying in its wake. A grounds-man who was carefully tending to the driveway with a rake looked rather balefully at the mess Rodger's car had made, and moved to re-arrange the pebbles he had disturbed. Rodger flashed him a grin as he bounced up the steps to the house, rather liking the irritation he could feel radiating from the man. *Good for the servants to know their place in the world*, thought Rodger.

"Rodger, old man!" cried his father, wandering down the stairs and looking like he was already a little tipsy, "good to see you, good drive down was it?"

Rodger sighed inwardly. His father's obsession with the route anyone took to his property never failed to amaze and bore him. Perhaps it was because no matter what route was cited, it would always be the wrong one in his father's eyes. It wasn't even as though there was much choice in the matter, but no matter what, whatever route he described would be the wrong one. His father did like to try to lord it over anyone, it was endlessly irritating. And, true to form, as soon as he told his father what roads he had taken, he was rewarded with a *tsk*.

"*Tsk, tsk*, son," said his father, waggling a finger at Rodger, "there are always delays on *that* road."

"Yes, Father… well, I'll know for next time, won't I?"

"Life's all about learning, boy," grinned his father, clapping him on the back, "but you can always learn a thing or two from your old man, can't you?" He pulled Rodger inside and leaned in to his ear. "Good thing you're here, son," he said gravely. "Will's been trying to bend my ear about some new plan he has… wanting to turn this old place into some kind of greeny-weany hippy retreat." The old man scowled slightly at the thought of his younger son. "Says there's money in it, but if he thinks that I'm going to hand over the family estate to have a bunch of bloody new-agers running all over it with their dreadlocks and crystals, he's got another thing coming…"

Rodger smiled and clapped a hand to the old man's back, "don't worry, *Pater*," he said gamely, "you know that you and I have always thought alike. I wouldn't let anything like that happen to the old place."

"True, true." Rodger's father clapped him hard on the back once more and took him into the house. The family pile was a massive construction, mainly Tudor, but with additions from many ages tacked onto it as well. With an impressive ten bedrooms, huge kitchens, several rooms for entertaining and with a large stable block attached, it was a sizeable estate. His parents had paid through the nose for it to be restored and decorated. The dark brown wood of antique furniture sat comfortably near restored record players and huge black televisions in the living room and the snug. The great stairs which ran up the middle of the entrance hall were polished to perfection with beeswax and lavender. Small and expensive bits of pottery were displayed here and there on little stands, and oil paintings of country scenes, which Rodger detested, lined the walls. Standing before the stairs, Rodger could almost smell the cash along with the polish… he breathed it in, relishing every high and low note. Soon enough, all this would be his, depending, of course, on how fast his father could be persuaded to shuffle off the old mortal coil.

"Rodger!" exclaimed his mother, wafting towards him in a cloud of peach-coloured dress and overpowering perfume. She kissed each of his cheeks and beamed at him. "Are you well? You look a little thin…"

Again, Rodger sighed to himself. His mother was made of generous proportions, and always seemed to think that everyone should look as she did; as though they had consumed enough food to feed the whole estate in one day. His mother was a well-meaning woman, but her true loves in life were food, and her horses, which she rode out each day from her stables. Aside from those things, she seemed to take little interest in the rest of life. When the time came, and his father died, Rodger would see his mother placed in a nice rest home, far away, where she could eat to her heart's content, and not bother him any further.

"Will and Henners are already here, then?" he asked, looking at the bags dumped at the foot of the stairs.

"Oh yes," his mother said vaguely, as though she had put her two younger children down somewhere and had forgotten where, "they arrived earlier."

"How are they?"

"Well," his mother said, looking worriedly at her husband, "Henrietta says her course at university is boring, and she's thinking of giving it up, and Will has some new thoughts about the estate he wants to talk with your father about."

Rodger nodded, not really caring. His sister, Henrietta, the youngest in the family at only twenty-three, was in her first year at her second university, embarking on her second attempt at a degree. The first had been in Law, but it seemed that this had bored her silly, and she had given it up, only to enlist in a course in English Literature this year, which she was now, too, apparently finding boring. No wonder, thought Rodger, who would want to spend three years reading *books* for heaven's sake? Rodger was proud of the fact that he never read books, thinking them to be an antiquated and rather stuffy pastime. Will, the middle child, was only two years younger than Rodger, and had spent his time working as some sort of outward-bound activity instructor. Rodger shivered with disgust when Will had once disclosed his meagre salary to his brother. Why would someone want to spend so much time, making so little money? Will was one of those people who said that money wasn't everything, which made him a fool in Rodger's eyes.

His parents hustled him into the drawing room, chattering away at him. His father was going on about the yield of wheat and barley that year from the farms, and his mother rattling on about some horse who was going to be the next winner of the local show-jumping... Rodger nodded and smiled, fixing on his face a look of interest which he did not feel inside. *Just keep them happy, old boy*, he said to himself silently, *just keep them happy.*

As they passed the grand staircase something in the corner of Rodger's eye caught his attention. He turned his head slightly as he was ushered through for drinks in the drawing room... what was that? For a moment it had looked as though something small and brown scuttled along the doorway of the billiard room. His father caught his eye. "What is it?" he asked.

Rodger shook his head, "I thought I saw... no," he smiled and turned back, shaking his head, "it was nothing, Pater, let's go in. I've been thinking about having a drop of your single malt all the way from London."

His father laughed and clapped him on the back, drawing him to the fine selection of spirits on the table. As he sipped the warm, amber-coloured liquid, Rodger quite forgot the little thing he had seen scuttle along the floor.

*

Later, they all assembled for dinner. His parents liked to make a show of things when all the family were together, or when there were guests, or when it was a Tuesday... the long table in the dining room was laid out as though they were in Gosford Park or Downton Abbey; long white table cloths, sparkling silverware, and long pale candles with the light of their flames bobbing in the soft shadows. Rodger took his place at the side of his father, the place of the next-most-important-member-of-the-family, and smiled at his brother and sister. Although the parents didn't quite go in for the whole frog-suit with coat and tails for dinner, it wasn't far off. Rodger had on one of his best suits, as did his father. His mother was wearing something which looked like she had borrowed it from the Queen; a long-flowing mass of powder blue, making her look like a frothy wave on a sunny sea. His sister was wearing a long black dress, and a miserable expression, and his brother Will, always the odd one out of the family, was wearing a shirt and trousers. *Didn't even bother with a tie and jacket,* thought Rodger. Rodger disapproved generally of his brother, but couldn't help but feel a little gnawing sense of jealously as he looked on Will's tanned face and arms, and the carefree manner he seemed to hold himself with. His brother had been the one who got the better share of the looks in the family, such as they were. It made Rodger a little jealous, but then he thought of how much more money he had than his brother and all was well again. After all, what could looks get you that money could not? Women went for men with money every time, over men with looks… just look at all the rich old goats in the world, like Hugh Hefner and Rupert Murdoch… women didn't flock to them for their *looks*, did they?

"Well, family, now that we are all gathered, I would like to announce that I have something to talk to all of you about during this holiday," his father said as the plates from the first course of salad leaves and tiny black pudding slices from the estate's own pigs, which Rodger had found rather gritty and slimy, were taken away. All of the family looked at him; even Rodger's sister, Henrietta, managed to get a spark of some interest into her eyes. "The time comes, in every man's life," his father continued and Rodger forced a smile of interest onto his face to combat the inner misery of listening to his father talk once more, about his *legacy*… "The time comes in every man's life when he must think about his *legacy*…" his father went on, true to form. Rodger felt his spirits sink. He must have heard this speech or various variations on it, a million times. His father's *legacy*… it was as though his father thought he was a king…

"What we leave behind for our children, and who will make the most of what we leave behind," his father droned on. Rodger stifled a yawn and smiled at his mother, who was looking at her husband with wrapt adoration. *One day*, Rodger thought, *I need to find a wife like that… one who simply accepts everything I say, and worships me for it.* Women like his mother were getting harder and harder to come by these days. It was as though they all wanted to *think* for themselves, and have jobs or something, rather than just accepting hand-outs of cash and getting on with running a house, like the good old days. Rodger sighed; perhaps he'd been born too late to find his ideal woman. But then he thought of those rich old men again, with those beautiful, brainless wives. There were still some of those rare creatures out there in the world, he thought with pleasure.

"I grew this place up from nothing," continued his father, "when we first took hold of it, it was a mess of a place... and now, it's our *castle*." He beamed out at the family, ignoring a sigh of exasperation from Henrietta at the far end of the table. "And I want to make sure that one of you takes it on, and does what's best for it."

"As you know, Father, I have many ideas on new ways that we could use the estate to make money," Will cut in, leaning forward on those tanned arms and looking intently at his father. "The retreat ideas I've been working on... I've made a business plan for them, costed it all up... I really think that this kind of thing..."

He didn't get any further. His father interrupted him. "William, I am not letting a bunch of hippy leftie-loonies run amuck about the place with glow-sticks and marijuana cigarettes," said his father, his face glowing with anger. He also pronounced 'marijuana' as though it was "marrrry-you-anna", which Rodger thought was vaguely amusing.

Will's face darkened. "It wouldn't be like that, Father," he said, "as I've tried to tell you. Spiritual retreats are just one of many platforms we could try here... there's writers' retreats, there's riding... think of how many people could come and enjoy the horses, Mother!"

"The horses are not there to be *enjoyed*," said his mother stiffly, looking at her husband as though she was a Stepford Wife before answering. "They are there to be ridden by qualified riders, not by all and sundry."

Will sighed and sat back, running his hand through his (Rodger thought) rather long hair. "Look, I'm just saying that there are many other ways to make money from the estate, and help with the up-keep," he said. "I think you should consider some of my ideas, just take a look at my business plan, Father…"

"I would like to hear what Rodger has to say," said their father stiffly, looking at Rodger.

"Oh, of course, let's all hear what Rodger has to say," spat Henrietta, sitting back and folding her arms as though she was four rather than twenty-three. "Never mind what the *girl* in the family has to say."

"You'll get your turn at the end, dear," their mother smiled at her daughter as though that made everything alright. Henrietta stared at her mother as though she was a creature from another planet.

"Well, I believe, as you know, Father, in the traditional ways," said Rodger with a smile at his mother and father. "If I were to be left the estate, I would of course continue with the farming and the stables, as they are…. Perhaps buying more land and expanding the estate, but always working on the same model." He grinned at his father, "if something ain't broke…"

"Exactly!" his father beamed at him. "We'll all talk more, over this festive season, but I would be most assured to think of my work, my legacy, continuing and progressing as it is… ah, venison, my favourite."

As the main course was brought in, the table returned to general chit-chat: Rodger informed his mother of all the things he ate on a regular basis as a balm to her fears that he was growing thin; Will tried gamely to engage his father in discussion about his projects once again, and was roundly ignored, and Henrietta picked at her food with an expression of disgust, eating the vegetables and ignoring the meat.

"Are you not hungry, dear?" asked their mother, finally noting when the plates were taken away that her daughter hadn't eaten a great deal.

"I told you last year; I'm a vegetarian," said Henrietta.

"Did you? I don't remember you saying anything like that," said their mother.

"They'll be no vegetarians in my house!" bellowed their father, "pasty-faced, whey-cheeked, greeny-weanies... no, sir!"

"Well there is one in your house, Father!" shouted his sister, getting up from the table and casting a dark look at her father. "So you'll just have to deal with that!" and with that, Henrietta walked out of the dining room.

The table sat stunned. It was a situation none of them were entirely prepared for; a walk-out from dinner was unheard of... Rodger covered the silence by asking his father about his investments, something which he never tired of talking about.

He regretted that choice when the old man went on, at great length, about the subject right through dessert and into the study where they stood with brandies and coffee by the huge fireplace. Rather than listen to the old man, Rodger let his mind wander pleasurably over all the things he would buy when he had control of the estate and its money... a boat... a cruise... a good house in London... ah, the possibilities.

As Rodger's mind wandered these pretty paths, he sat back in the chair, his brandy nestled in one hand. His father, Will and his mother were all sitting on the other side of the fire, and he was sitting overlooking the door. As he looked up at his father, still rattling away about his portfolio, his gaze was caught by something… something in the hallway… something small and brown, which looked as though it was bobbing towards the room. Rodger sat up and stared out of the doorway. The entrance hall was dark, lit with only a few lamps, but he was sure he could see, something… something coming towards the room.

The thing was bobbing along, moving rather like some small kind of vermin, and Rodger wondered for a moment if his parents had rats in the house. But then, he saw it was also walking, or lolloping strangely, lopsided, awkward… it was as though the thing, whatever it was, was wounded. It lurched and staggered towards the doorway, and as it came into the light of the room, Rodger saw a strange and twisted body, made of brown fur and red, raw flesh. It bobbed into the doorway and Rodger jumped out of his seat, letting out a strangled cry of fear and disgust as he saw its face; on one side, it was the face of a wild rabbit, with one black eye, bright, sparkling and keen in a wealth of brown fur. On the other side, it was a mangled mess of red flesh, blood oozing from one empty socket, which seemed to stare at him from a distorted mass of raw muscle and bone. Rodger's brandy fell to the floor, and his crystal glass bounced across the heavy sheepskin rug. His hand lifted, pointing shakily at the door way where the half-dead creature stared balefully at him, and a strangled cry of horror and fear rose from his mouth.

The others leapt up, turning and looking to where Rodger pointed, but as they did so, the creature of blood and raw flesh seemed to dissipate, blending into the shadows like a whiff of smoke… They all turned and stared at him, but Rodger could not move. He was paralysed with fear.

"What on earth was it, old boy?" his father asked with a nervous laugh. But Rodger just gaped at the doorway, wondering if he was imagining things, or if he had truly seen the awful creature. In the end, his brother walked to him and lowered his shaking, pointing hand himself, and then nodded at him. "You must have nodded off there, Rodg," his brother said carefully, "it's been a long drive, and a long day... why don't we all call it a night?"

Rodger stared at his brother as though he didn't know who he was for a moment, and then looked back at the doorway. The creature, the thing, whatever it was, was gone. He looked back at his brother and passed a shaking hand over his face which was wet with sweat. He nodded to Will. "Yes..." he said, and tried to let out a laugh which sounded more like a cough, "yes... it's been a long day, I must have just, nodded off, like you say, Wills." Rodger turned to his father who was regarding him with a worried face. "I'll say goodnight, then," he said and left the room without stopping to kiss his mother, or say another word.

As he left the room and almost ran for the stairs, Rodger heard his father mutter, "well, that was odd." But he didn't have time to think about that now. He just wanted to get somewhere, safe...

Rodger showered in the adjacent bathroom to his room. A long, hot shower. He put his face under the flowing water of the shower and put his hands to the wall, just letting the water rush over his face and body. What had he seen? He was sure that he had seen something, but then, it had vanished when the others turned around... what was it? It had looked like a rabbit. Vaguely, Rodger remembered the rabbit he had killed driving here... but that wasn't possible, was it? He almost laughed; he was being haunted by the spirit of a road-kill rabbit, was he? The thought was preposterous. It must be all the stress of work... all those targets he had to meet and people he had to manage. He had heard that stress could make strange things happen to a person, but had never experienced it himself. Perhaps this was just a manifestation of the stress of the job. Yes, that must be it.

Rodger stood in the shower for some time, even after assuring himself that what he had seen was just a manifestation of stress. He did not want to admit even to himself that he did not want to open his eyes in case he saw the rabbit again.

*

Rodger finally climbed into the huge king-size bed with its faux four-poster look, and tried to draw the curtains around him. He felt as though he needed to be in a smaller space, even than just the bedroom. He needed to be able to close himself in, protect himself. Again, he almost shrugged off the idea as ridiculous… to protect himself from what? The rabbit? But the feeling of fear and unease would not abate, and although the curtains were really more for decoration than actual use, he succeeded in pulling them about the bed, with only the slightest of cracks in them at his sides and in front of him. He thought about taking some time on Twitter, but could not think of anything inspiring to say to his followers. Eventually, he just turned out the light, and lay there, trying to gather his thoughts of the day and what it all meant.

Perhaps this was a sign, a sign that he was working too hard, and needed to take some time off. When he got back to work, he would book in a holiday, go somewhere warm, and leave the job behind for a bit. He had not realized that it was having such an effect on his nerves… but obviously it was. Yes, he needed a holiday; that much was clear.

As Rodger lay there, waiting for sleep to take him, he became aware of a little noise in the room. Soft and hardly noticeable at first, it seemed to grow, creeping into his awareness and gnawing at his already frayed nerves. It was a scuttling sound… the sound of little claws tapping on hard-wood floors…. Something was in the room, and it was moving about.

Rodger sat up with a start, his hand darting from between the curtains and fumbling for the bedside lamp. Light flooded the room, and Rodger leapt to the edge of the curtains, peeking from the gap with wide eyes. Sweat popped out in little beads on his forehead, and he felt his spine shiver with fear. He looked up and down the room, but could see nothing out of the ordinary. He sat back, staring to shake a little, and unwilling to turn off the light again. As he sat back against the Egyptian cotton and plush pillows, the noise started again. A scuttling, scraping, creeping noise... he could definitely hear it this time. He sat up again, his breathing rasping, his hands grasping at the bedspread. He jumped forward and grasped at the curtains before him, pulling them back even as he leapt... and then Rodger fell forwards, his legs tangled in the thick bedcovers. He tumbled with a cry from the foot of the bed, one hand still grasping the curtains which ripped from their hooks with a series of loud pops. He landed on the hard polished floor in a tumble of bedcovers and bed curtain, limbs and joints bouncing heavily on the floor. Rodger cried out in pain and confusion, suddenly finding himself in a jumbled mess on the floor. There was a shout from another room, near his own, but he paid it little heed, for at that moment, as he struggled to free himself from the bed sheets over his head, he saw the one bright and keen eye of the rabbit watching him from under the desk opposite his bed. Rodger screamed loudly as he saw the creature start its lopsided, haunting hop towards him once more... its bloody eye staring at him balefully as it lolloped towards him, fresh, red blood running down the raw and twisted flesh on its face... Rodger let out another scream, and twisted violently in the covers, trying to free himself as the rabbit hopped towards him...

The door to Rodger's room flew open, and in ran Will and Henners, each in bedclothes. Henners was brandishing a black fire poker in her hands. Both Rodger's siblings stopped as they entered the room; shouts of concern poised on their lips, they stopped and stared at the pile of bedcovers on the floor which contained the still-struggling Rodger.

"Rodger... old man... are you alright?" Will asked, walking forwards and pulling at the knotted bedcovers, only to stare in surprise at Rodger's white and terrified face within. "Did you have a bad dream or something?" he asked, staring at his brother. Will looked at Henrietta with concern, and she lowered the poker, looking at her eldest brother with a somewhat amused and puzzled frown.

Rodger looked wildly about him, twisting this way and that in the covers, looking rather like a caterpillar trying to free itself from a chrysalis without success. Henrietta stared harder at her brother, obviously wondering what he was doing, and then, to Rodger's amazement, started laughing.

"Rodger, what *are* you doing?" she asked, still giggling, poker in hand.

"The rabbit!" Rodger squawked, the words tumbling from his mouth. "The rabbit!"

Henrietta stopped laughing and stared at her older brother, was he going round the bend? "The rabbit?" she asked cautiously.

Rodger nodded furiously, only making himself look more and more ridiculous as the bed covers on his head bobbed up and down. He tried to point, but his arm got caught in part of the curtain. He looked, Wills thought, rather like a partially unwrapped escaped mummy…

Rodger's mother and father appeared at the doorway, looking in with slightly annoyed eyes. "What is all the noise about?" his father asked, standing barefoot in his blue and white striped pyjamas, and looking at each of them. When he saw Rodger on the floor, covered in blankets and curtain, he looked at his eldest son and heir and then at the others. "Were you three having a pillow fight?" he asked.

Will snorted slightly. "Don't you think we're a bit old for that, Father?" He nodded at Rodger on the floor. "We heard a noise from Rodger's room, thought there might be an intruder, but it seems that he must have had a dream and sleep-walked, or something." Wills trailed off, still looking worriedly at Rodger's white face he leant down and helped his brother from the mess of bed linen. "Just a dream, old man," he said reassuringly, "you must have just had a bad dream."

Rodger could only nod and climb gratefully from the covers as Will helped him out. He nodded, hearing Will's cooing, reassuring tone and melting into it. Under normal circumstances, he would have been annoyed by it. Now, it seemed to him as though Will's words and tone of comfort washed over him, soothing him. He nodded and leaned on his brother. "Yes," Rodger murmured. "Just a bad dream... I didn't realize I had nodded off..."

"Well, then," his father said, sounding unsure, "if that's all it was then I'll be back to bed then." He put a hand on his wife's shoulder. "Come on then, Poppy."

With a last look at her children, and a worried expression, their mother followed her husband back to their room. Henrietta watched them go and shook her head at Rodger. "Must have been quite a dream, Rodg," she said, still looking amused. "And about rabbits, no less."

With a little laugh, Henners turned on her heel and went back to her own room, leaving Will to help Rodger pile the dismantled curtains on the floor, and put the covers back on the bed.

"Are you sure you're alright, Rodg?" Wills asked, lingering at the door. "You've been acting a bit odd since you arrived... is everything alright, you know, at work and in life?"

Rodger sat down heavily on the edge of the bed, feeling very feeble and tired all of a sudden. He nodded to his brother. "I'm fine, Will," he said, his voice sounding entirely unconvincing. "I... think I might need a break from work, is all... been putting in a lot of hours... I might be suffering from stress, or something."

Will nodded like an aged sage. "Stress is the new disease of the working classes," he said.

"I'm not working class." Rodger was quickly on the defensive; even in this state he had no wish to be lumbered with that kind of title.

"Sorry… people that work, then," said Will with a smile. "There's no such thing as class anymore, old man, that's the old way of thinking. These days, a millionaire can become a pauper in a day, and an idiot can become a millionaire with one short clip on YouTube…. You're living in the past if you think it's all about what class you come from. Barriers are coming down all around us, and the world is changing faster than you think. It's all about *ideas* now… who has them, and who can use them."

Rodger nodded to his brother, wishing he would go away. No matter how scared he had been, or how confusing this night was turning out to be, he had little desire to be lectured by his younger brother, who clearly knew nothing.

Will puckered his lips a little, noting Rodger's annoyance at him. "Well, I'll be off then," he said. "Perhaps you *should* book some time off, Rodg, from work I mean. Have a holiday, relax a little… clearly something is not right."

Rodger nodded, passing a hand over his clammy forehead. "I thought just the same," he mumbled.

Will left the room, and Rodger climbed back into his messy bed, pulling the covers around him even though the warm room kept out the chill of the damp December air outside. He left the light on, on one side of the bed, but reached over and unplugged the light on the other side, taking it into his hands. If that damned rabbit made another appearance this night, then he would give it what for….

The adrenalin from his second scare of the evening flowed from his veins quickly, leaving him suddenly exhausted. Rodger fell asleep in his large bed, bathed in the steady light of the lamp at his side, and the second lamp cradled in his arms.

*

Rodger awoke from a fitful sleep, his dreams haunted by the glistening black eye of the rabbit and the sound of its claws scraping on wooden floors. As he blearily blinked his eyes at the grey-white light of the dawn stretching its fingers through the windows, his hands clutched compulsively at the lamp in his lap, bringing it upwards against his body, as though he was Arthur, and this was Excalibur...

Thoughts and memories of the past night came to him, flitting across his mind and appearing in broken, shattered images. The rabbit's face as his car had slammed into it... his father greeting him on the driveway... the vague glimpse of something moving across the doorway... his sister's discontented face at dinner... Will's tanned arms... and then, the sight of that black eye gleaming at him from the darkness.

Rodger began to shiver uncontrollably; he felt as though he might never be warm again. He gathered the bedcovers about him, pulling them to cover all of his skin, all of his body. He sank down into the covers and the lovely, plush bed, still clutching the lamp against him. Its hardness seemed reassuring. He was still shaking when he felt something move against his foot at the end of the bed. He jerked his leg backwards, and started trying to move into a sitting position, but the creature was too quick for him. It leapt from the end of the bed in one huge bound, and landed directly on his chest, lurching crazily from side to side. Its bloody eye and its good eye were both fixed on Rodger's face. Rodger let out a deep and strange noise of terror which carried on escaping from his mouth as though it would never stop. The rabbit rode Rodger's chest as he screamed, twisting his body and his head this way and that, trying to avoid the gaze of the creature. His hands flailed out, sweeping the air with the lamp, but to no avail. As Rodger continued to scream, he saw the lamp pass straight through the body of the rabbit, not once making contact. The rabbit continued to ride his chest, bobbing and weaving its little body, and never failing to stare at Rodger with its baleful eyes.

Rodger screamed a high-pitched scream of pure terror, and stumbled from the bed. Lashing this way and that through the air, he swung the heavy lamp at the rabbit. Stumbling backwards, Rodger hit the window, and managed to smash it with the swinging lamp. Glass flew over his shoulder, hitting his face and skin, but he didn't care. He held the lamp before him as though it was a sword, pointing it at the rabbit who still sat on the bed.

"You… you stay there!" he screamed at the rabbit and then, just for a moment, he thought he saw a glimmer of amusement in the rabbit's good eye.

"Stop it!" he screamed, "stop haunting me! You shouldn't have been on the road! Roads are for cars and cars are for roads!"

The rabbit, if it was capable of saying anything, did not respond but instead started to hop deliberately and slowly across the bed towards Rodger, one bloody leg dragging across the white cotton covers…

"Nooooooo!" screamed Rodger, skirting around the edge of the room, his back to the wall, facing the rabbit. As he ran around the edge of the room he knocked paintings from the walls and priceless antiques from shelves, but he didn't care. His bare feet were cut and bleeding from the shattered glass and porcelain on the floor, but he didn't notice the pain. All Rodger cared about now was getting out of this room and away from this rabbit.

"Stay away from me!" he screamed as he reached the door, but the rabbit continued to hop towards him. Rodger ran from the room, wielding the lamp in his hands. He ran past Will and Henrietta who stood staring at him from their respective doorways. He ran past his father and mother as they emerged, running and shouting with fear and concern from their own rooms. He ran past the housemaid at the top of the stairs, and as he dodged to try to avoid her, his foot caught on the edge of the long red carpet. For a moment, Rodger seemed to hover in mid-air at the top of the stairs. The lamp in his hands, his white pyjamas ripped and stained with blood, an expression of pure terror on his face... and then, time started again, and Rodger fell, faster than anyone could seem to imagine, down the stairs. The lamp flew out of his hands, hitting him on the head as he fell, and he landed, eventually, in a crumpled heap on the landing.

As the others reached him, Rodger was conscious, but whimpering. "Roads are for cars," he muttered over and over again. "Roads are for cars, not for rabbits."

"There, there, old man," his father said, patting Rodger's back and attempting to support his wife who had dissolved into tears at his side. Henrietta called for an ambulance and Will sat pale-faced, staring at Rodger on the landing. "We're going to get you some help, Rodg," Wills said, patting Rodger on the arm.

"Roads are for cars, not rabbits," Rodger said to Will, staring up at him with glassy, unfocused eyes.

"Yes... absolutely, Rodg," Will replied as though he was speaking to an old relative. "Roads are for cars, that's right..."

*

The ambulance came in amazingly short time, thought Will, considering it was Christmas Day. They seemed to take Rodger's high-pitched squeaking completely in their stride as they checked him over and then put him on their trolley to take him to the hospital. Will made sure he mentioned about

Rodger's problem with stress, and his odd behaviour of the night before, in case it was relevant. Henrietta and their mother went in the ambulance with Rodger to the hospital, and his father and Will were to follow behind.

As they stood, watching the ambulance up the drive, Will's father turned to him.

"Perhaps later, son," he said, staring at the ambulance with an odd expression, as though he was suddenly unsure of himself. "Perhaps, you could show me that business plan of yours?"

Will smiled at his father. "I'd be delighted," he said.

Old Man Symmonds

It all happened one Christmas when I was working part-time in a retail store in Plymouth. I won't name the store, or mention where it was on that cluttered high street. Suffice to say that it was a medium-sized store selling clothes and various bath stuffs, candles and useless ornaments, which people seem in such a rush to buy at Christmas. The store had a large front, and a back store room stuffed with old stock which we had been slowly sorting to bring out for the sales after Christmas. It was a nice enough place, but I did not want to be working in a retail store. I was not happy working there, but having encountered a new boss at my old job who was a complete nightmare to work under, I had left, and had been forced to find part time work whilst I searched for a new job.

It wasn't that I was incapable of using a till, or smiling at people who seemed to assume that just because you were standing behind a counter you must have fewer brain cells than them, which caused my dissatisfaction at my 'stop-gap' job, as my boyfriend Chris called it. It wasn't just the complete banality of the job: the constant tidying of clothes and candles brought about because people couldn't seem to return things to the right rack; it wasn't the people who asked where the toilets were, despite there being a thousand signs for them about the store; it wasn't having to be unfailingly polite to impolite people… it was the feeling that I had been forced to leave something I was good at, that I enjoyed, because I could not stand to work under my new manager.

I had been an office manager and sometime bookkeeper; dull, you might think, but I loved my old job. I liked to keep order. I liked my neat spreadsheets, my well-filed folders and the satisfaction of meeting the goals I set myself. I liked the fact that I knew the business inside out, and could answer any and all questions to new staff, or people enquiring about this and that. Perhaps I was a big fish in a little pond, but if so I had been bathing happily in those waters, and had no desire to move elsewhere. My old boss, the one I had before the one who came in to ruin my life, was a lovely guy; he was kind and calm, always listened to your opinion and talked problems over with you. He was secure in his competence for the role, and loved it when new ideas came in, even from the seemingly unchanging sector of the office admin. I had listened to friends complain bitterly about bosses who lorded it over them, about bosses who had gone in for humiliation and bullying, and I had thought how fortunate I was to have such an amazing boss… and fortune I was… for a while.

It was when Keith retired, and the new boss from Head Office arrived, that my life at work became a nightmare. My new boss was a woman, and she came highly recommended, so Keith thought that we'd all be happy under her. He went on to his retirement with plans about growing artichokes and damsons in his allotment, and we thought that since this person came with Keith's approval it would all work out well. I even looked forward to having a female boss… but what did not occur to me in my dazed ideal of such an idea, is the truth that in a world of increasingly equal opportunities, some women are just as capable of being terrible bosses as men…

At first, it was all little things; she had an odd, sporadic way about her, seeming to be happy and chatty one day, and the next upbraiding us for talking in the office during "quiet time". She seemed ill at ease when I brought problems to her, as though she had little understanding of what I was talking about, and when I solved those problems without her, it seemed rather as though she was taking the credit for *my* work when they were brought up in team meetings. We had occasional, sporadic one-on-one meetings where she would tell me about her problems with the company and I would sympathise, and then when I tried to talk to her about my problems, such as they were, a blank look would come over her face, and she would go strangely quiet… I quickly realised that the reason for this was because she understood nothing about my job, nor it seemed about any of the others who worked there.

It was unnerving to think that the person who directly oversaw me understood nothing about what I did, or the timescales I worked to. She kept trying to pile work on me at times when I had other, more urgent tasks to do, and if I tried to point that out then I would get a look which seemed to say "well, if you can't do your job..." I also found out that she had started to complain about me to other staff. Rather than confront me directly about any problems, she spent time talking about me behind my back. She did the same about others to me, at first, and then stopped when I told her that she should confront them honestly in their reviews about such matters... apparently nothing like that was ever likely to happen. Direct confrontation was not her way.

"Don't worry about it, love," said Chris when I came home each night bubbling over with anger like a boiling stew-pot on a stove. "Just keep your head down and do the work, everyone has crap bosses... and if you don't want to do it anymore then leave, there are other jobs out there."

"I like my job!" I said, close to tears as I threw my bag down on the floor and a dozen pens, pencils, scraps of paper and stray tampons flew out of it as it hit the floor. "I want Keith back!"

"If wishes were horses..." said Chris, shaking his head and giving me a hug. I nodded against his shoulder.

"I know, I know... I can't bring my old boss back... but Carol is such a nightmare, Chris, you have no idea."

"At least she's not a complete psycho like my boss," he laughed over my head. "I honestly think one day I'll come in and find him hiding a body under his desk... he even looks like that guy off that film."

"Christian Bale," I replied, my voice muffled against his chest and Chris nodded.

"That's him. How do you always know what I mean?"

I smiled up at him and kissed him, feeling better for the comfort of his arms about me. "I can read minds."

"Can you read mine now?" He pulled me closer, kissing my neck.

I lost my anger, easily distracted in bed by my boyfriend that night, but even if I could forget Carol at night, in the safety of home, I couldn't forget her at work. It just got worse and worse. She piled impossible amounts of work on to me, until I was sure that I was in fact doing *her* job for her, and made snide comments about my lack of progress in front of the others. Every time I tried to talk to her about my problems with her timescales, or unrealistic expectations of me, she just seemed to phase out, staring past me as though I wasn't even there. I felt myself growing depressed; waking up at three a.m. worrying about everything I had to do the next day. My appetite faltered at home, and I started to pick at my lunch at my desk in an effort to keep up with the workload. Because I never seemed to get to the top of my pile of work, I seemed to never achieve anything, and that only made me more depressed. And I had no ownership over anything, no power, no control. Carol took credit for everything I did, and monitored all my work, even my emails, to a point where I felt as though I might snap at any moment, and just go nuts at work.

"You need to *leave*, Hayley," Chris said after another night where I had spent perhaps two hours complaining bitterly and at length about Carol to him. He sighed and stroked my hair back from my face as we sat on the sofa with me curled about him. "You *are* good at your job," he said, "but there are other places you could transfer those skills to and work in another office."

"How do I know it wouldn't be like this one?"

"You don't, but you do know that it wouldn't be *this* one, wouldn't you?" he said with a smile.

"I've worked there since I left uni," I sighed, "I'd be sad to leave the others in the office."

"You can still see them, love" — he stroked my hair again — "but this isn't good for you. Your job has become toxic, and it's poisoning you. Life doesn't have to be like that. I'm not saying you'd get a boss as good as Keith, but maybe you'd find one who is better than Carol…. And besides," he grinned at me, "can you imagine what her face would be like if you handed in your resignation? If your suspicions are correct, and you are doing all her work as well as yours, then she's stuffed when you leave!"

I laughed. "It might be worth doing, just to see that!"

We laughed about it, but I thought about it more and more. And more and more I liked the idea of leaving and making a fresh start somewhere else. Chris was right; there were other offices, there were other jobs. Why should I let this one woman ruin my life? I updated my CV and started looking around, but perhaps it was because I had leaving in my head, or perhaps it was because I had already somewhat given up on my old job, but something in me started to push to leave earlier, to leave *now*. The urge to snap at Carol, or to hit her, I hadn't quite decided which, was wild within me, and I began to think that I might well get myself fired if I continued as I was. I spoke to Chris, and he supported the idea.

"I can always get a temporary post whilst I job-hunt," I nodded, "and I'll get the rest of my holiday pay when I leave."

"We've got some saved, love," he said. "I think you should just go ahead. Give Carol a month's notice, and then be done with it. That way you'll be able to see the light at the end of the tunnel... and you might well find another post before you leave."

So I did it. I wrote my letter, saying little about why I was leaving, just that I had decided to move on, walked into Carol's office, and handed it to her, then I walked out again, feeling my heart pulse with excitement and my head spin a little. I was as elated as I was scared. I had worked in this office for almost six years and had thought I'd probably continue to do so for the foreseeable future. When I was happy here, I had not had any desire to leave. But when I became unhappy, the place had closed around me like a trap. Suddenly, I felt as though I was able to breathe again.

Carol didn't come to me to talk to me about my resignation. She sent me an email saying that she would be sorry to see me go, but she would start advertising for my job immediately. I read it and smiled, *of course* she would need a replacement ASAP; she needed someone to do her work for her so that Head Office didn't notice for a while longer that she was incapable of doing anything herself. Word spread through the office that day, and I suddenly seemed to be the focus of a lot of smiles, and a lot of confidences bursting out of people.

"I've drafted *my* resignation, too," whispered Mona to me in the stationery cupboard. "But I have to find another job first... do you have anything lined up?"

I shook my head. "I'll find something during my notice period," I whispered back, "and if not, I'll just work in a bar, or do retail... I can't stand staying here any longer."

She giggled. "I know what you mean," she said. "Carol is a *total* fruitcake, do you know she forgot to tell me something about the King account, and then told me that she *had* told me and that *I* must have forgotten? And she asked me to send her my spreadsheets on another account, changed stuff around, and saved over the original... she got it all wrong, of course! It was such a mess, took me ages to sort it out when she gave it back... and then she ticked me off for handing it in late! It's enough; I'm gone as soon as I can find something else."

I nodded. "I know just what you mean," I said. But unlike Mona, I wasn't willing to wait.

During that last month, Carol did her utmost to make my life a misery. She phased in between being overtly sad, in front of everyone else, to see me going, to criticizing everything I did. I went on a few interviews, but couldn't find anything at that time which I thought I'd be happy with; I was either too qualified or not quite qualified enough.

"I'm going to get a temporary job in a shop or something," I said to Chris as we watched TV one evening. "And I might do a course; get my AAT, before I apply for other jobs. I should be able to get a higher paid job if I get the qualification. I know everything I need to know to do it... I just never took the course when I was with Keith, because I didn't think I'd need it."

"We can cut into our savings a bit, and take it easy on any spending," mused my ever-practical boyfriend. "With my wage we can meet the rent and anything you bring in we can use for the bills and the groceries. If this course would help you get a better paid job, one you'd be happy doing, then you should do it."

So I applied for sales positions in various stores, it was pretty easy to get a job in retail since Christmas was looming and the seasonal spending madness was about to begin. I had worked in a big department store to pay my way through university, so I knew the drill, and just needed a bit of re-training on the new EPOS systems on tills and suchlike. I applied for an AAT course and was accepted, and started to think how nice it would be to be a student again for a while. I could work part time and study the rest, and when all this was done, I could apply for a job with an accountancy firm and work my way up the ladder. It would present fresh challenges, and I rather liked that idea. In fact I was feeling quite positive right up until my last day at work when Carol gave me my reference.

She hadn't found anyone for my position, and had actually asked me to stay on for a while longer, but I had refused, saying I was starting a new job and my course, so I couldn't continue with the job. With that in mind, rather than fill my post with a temp, which might have been suitable, she took all my work and handed it out to the other staff in the offices. Poor Martin, who had only come on that year, thought that he was going to buckle under the workload he had been handed. Mona looked positively wild with restrained annoyance. Carol spoke in a team meeting about the possibility of keeping this arrangement, to save on wages… much to the horror of everyone in the office. Because she had no understanding of my job, she didn't seem to grasp that office manager was, and always would be, a full-time role.

I felt bad, but what could I do? I had made a choice, and I had to see it through, even if it meant leaving friends I had worked with for a long time in the shit. I reasoned that this was Carol's choice, not mine. She was the manager, not me… it was up to her to actually have a clue about the office she was running.

And then she gave me my reference. When I opened it, I stared at it for a moment, thinking there had been a mistake. But then I realized there wasn't. It contained the dates I had worked here for, and my job title with a few basic responsibilities, and that was it. Employers aren't allowed to give a bad reference by law, but all new employers know what it means when they are handed a reference with just the dates of work on them. It means the old employer had nothing good to say. It means that *this is a person you should think twice about employing.*

Carol was trying to scupper me, even now, even when I was almost out of her clutches, she still couldn't just let me go with grace. She was trying to sink the HMS Hayley. I couldn't quite believe it.

"I'd like to talk to you about my reference, Carol," I said, walking into her office with my cheeks flaming with anger.

She looked up from her desk and smiled her annoying fake smile. "Yes?"

"It only has a few lines about my responsibilities," I said, floundering in my rage.

"It has everything on it which I have observed of your work and competence over the past few months," she said breezily, "and I won't be changing anything on it."

"I've worked here for six years. I *ran* this office!" I almost hissed the words through my teeth. Around the office I could see other members of the staff looking up at us and trying to hide their interest. I didn't care really. I wanted people to know what she was doing to me.

"But I have only been observing your work for the past few months," she said with another, wider smile. "So I can only note on here what I have seen for myself, can't I?"

Spiteful little cow! She was doing all this just to get back at me for resigning! I drew myself up and stared at her, then took the letter and placed it on her desk. "You can keep your reference, Carol," I said calmly even though my hands were shaking with rage. "I don't need it. I'll ask Keith Matthews for a reference, and he'll be sure to give me one that adequately represents all that I did for this firm in the last six years." I paused and looked her in the eyes. "After all, at least *he* had an idea of what went on in this firm, unlike some."

I turned and walked away, back to my desk. It was my last day; there was nothing that she could do to me now. Although anger still ran through my blood, I knew that in fact Carol was going to be far worse off than I was. I was going on to new things, I was capable and practical. Carol had no idea what she was doing, and she had just split my job between five people, four of whom I knew were thinking of leaving, because of her. Eventually, she would rid this place of all the good staff who worked here, and only when she found herself surrounded by new people, or temps, would she understand that she would have to either do some work, get a clue, or leave for another post.

I packed up my desk into a little box, said goodbye to the friends I had there, and left. I did not say good-bye to Carol. As I walked out the door, I looked up at the old Queen Anne building where our offices were, and I felt sad looking at the warm red-bricked walls shining in the early December sunshine, thinking of all the good times when I had loved working there. The days when I had woken up feeling eager to get to work, feeling a sense of satisfaction in my working day, feeling as though I was achieving something. But this place was no longer like that for me; I had to take a new path to regain that feeling, and I was about to embark on it.

I walked off down the street with a little skip in my step. Perhaps it was just adrenalin from returning my rubbish reference to Carol, perhaps it was the excitement and fear of trying something new in my life, but whatever it was, I felt quite euphoric as I came home that night, and more so when Chris opened a bottle of bubbly wine to celebrate my liberation from the boss from hell.

"Freeeeedom!" Chris shouted as he clinked his glass with mine in a noisy, if passable impression of *Braveheart*.

"You may take our spreadsheets, but you'll never take our Freeedom!" I cried back, and drank, feeling the bubbles go straight to my head. "Uck!" I said when I finally tasted the stuff, "rather harsh on the way down?"

Chris laughed and topped up my glass. "Can't afford the good stuff for a while, my love," he grinned, "but don't worry, we'll come out the other side in a better place!"

The euphoria I felt at having left Carol behind was marvellous, but temporary. I did sometimes think of the office and of her as I started my new job, being trained by someone younger than me who seemed infinitely bored by absolutely everything that she instructed me in. The feeling of satisfaction at no longer being in my old job, and especially in not having to see Carol, was immense, but it didn't make up for having to work in retail again. I had forgotten how much I had hated it when I was at university; but I kept reminding myself, it was a temporary job, and when the AAT course started in January, I'd have something to be working towards, a sense of achievement and satisfaction in life. *Just hang on for now*, I said to myself, *and it will all work out in the end.*

Easier said than done, sometimes, but I tried to keep it in mind.

My new job wasn't too hard really, but it seemed to weigh heavily on me. I resented it, resented Carol for having pushed me into it. My course felt a long way off as I listened to the relentlessly cheerful music which played over and over in the shop in the run-up to Christmas. I helped customers, I took money, I put things in bags and gift-wrapped candles and clothes, all with a fixed smile on my face. My new boss, Kate, was a nice woman, and the other girls I worked with were friendly enough, but I was unhappy. I tried to put it all behind me, but found myself having muttered conversations with an imaginary Carol; conversations where I was a lot more honest and forthright than I had ever dared to be in the office. It is the way of such things, I suppose, to be braver in your own imagination than you are in real life.

I tried my best, and to be fair, my best was better than the best of some of the girls who worked in the shop. Clearly bored and unengaged with the job, they took minimum wage to mean minimum work, and spent a lot of time hiding in the back, consulting their mobiles about the status of their friends on social media. I kept my phone switched off at work, and tried to put myself into the tasks at hand, however boring they were. Kate seemed to notice this, and praised me for it. She asked about my plans after the Christmas period, and I was honest about studying for my AAT with plans about going on eventually to become an accountant. She didn't seem to take such news badly and even seemed to expect it to a certain degree. "There are few lifers," she said, grinning gamely at me, "apart from me, but then, this is my store and it's a labour of love." She smiled at me and I nodded.

"It's a lovely place," I said, even though I didn't really think so.

"There weren't many people who would take it on," she said. "When the old store was here… it used to be a hardware shop… and when the old boss died it passed through hand after hand, but no one stayed on for long," she smiled, "I got it for a steal, you know, because they had such trouble letting it."

I frowned at Kate. "Why should that be? It's in prime position on the high street."

She nodded, and a closed look came over her face. "Well, there were problems with damp, and… other things," she said and then tailed off. "Look, I need someone to close up tonight. I have to go to the bank and run a few errands… would you be willing? Stacey would be here until six, but if you could close up, well, you'd really be doing me a favour, and there'd be overtime in it for you?"

I nodded glumly. I didn't want to stay here longer, my shift was due to end at three, but we could really do with the money. "I'll do it," I said.

Kate nodded and smiled. "Good," she said. "If you could close the shop up at six when Stacey goes, and then just tidy the store and start sorting the back room stock before you go? It's such a mess back there and I really need it sorted before the Christmas rush really begins next week… we never have time to do anything after that! If you take an hour back there, but make sure you leave by seven p.m., won't you?" Her voice sounded suddenly anxious as she asked me to leave by seven, and I nodded to her, thinking that she must not want to have to pay for more overtime than that.

"I'd like to be home by eight anyway," I said.

"Make sure you leave by *seven*," she insisted, and then smiled at me. "I know this is only a temp job for you, Hayley, but I do like the way you approach the job. It's rare to find someone who really tries, you know?"

I smiled at her and nodded. We got on with the rest of the day, and as Kate was leaving at four, she turned to me again. "Make sure you leave by seven," she insisted again.

"I promise," I said.

*

When Stacey left at six, we locked up the takings and the float in the safe at the back of the store. As she collected her bag and jacket she turned to me, "Aren't you coming?" she asked.

I shook my head. "Kate wanted me to stay until seven and do a little stock sorting in the back."

She frowned deeper, and looked around her, as though she was suddenly scared of something. "Make sure you leave by seven *on the dot*," she said.

I shook my head and laughed. "What is it with the stroke of seven in this place?" I asked. "Do Santa and all his little elves come out at one minute past?"

I expected her to at least crack a smile, but she shook her head at me again. "Make sure you're out by *seven*," she said and motioned me to the door where she showed me how to pull down the outdoor shutters and how to lock and unlock the store from the inside. "By seven, don't forget," she said again. She looked as though she was about to say something else, but then just shook her head and walked away into the drizzle covering the grey high street. I watched her go with a slightly confused mind, but shrugged it off and went back inside. I shivered a little as I walked in from the rain outside and back into the warmth, locked the door, and made my way to the back of the store to start sorting through the old stock for the January sales.

Whilst I was back there, cleaning and packing half-full boxes of candles into full boxes, and chucking out the empty ones, I got quite lost in yet another imaginary conversation with Carol. I punctuated my words by slicing through the boxes with a knife as I pressed them flat for recycling, and lost track of the time as I did so.

"But I can only evaluate the skills I have seen from you, can't I, Hayley?" I said in my best squeaky Carol impression. *"I can only assess what I've seen...* as though she could see anything past that great big head of hers..."

As I went on with my Carol impression, a noise at the front of the store hauled me up short. I stopped throwing the cardboard onto the pile I was making and looked up. What was that? It sounded like footsteps in the store, as though someone was walking about... I had locked the door, hadn't I? There wasn't a customer out there, was there?

I threw the box I was holding onto the rather vast pile I had made and looked about me for a moment. I hadn't realised how much I had done... how long had I been here? I looked at my watch; it was half past seven. I really had to be going. Chris was out with his friends tonight, staying over at a mate's house in Truro to watch the game, so it wasn't like he'd be waiting for me, but I had wanted to take a long bath and watch a historical drama I could never convince him to watch with me on Netflix. I had been looking forward to a quiet evening at home with a glass of wine, watching men stride about in doublets… I brushed myself down and strode to the door of the stock room; if there was someone out there then they would have to come back to shop tomorrow. I walked towards the door, fixing my polite-customer-face on. But as I had almost reached the door, it slammed backwards with a huge whoosh and a crash, causing me to start and stop where I was. My hand remained outstretched, paused in its place reaching out for the handle, but every muscle and every drop of blood in my body seemed to freeze in place.

"Hello?" I said in a wavering voice, wondering if the door had slammed shut in some draught which I couldn't feel, or if the person I had heard in the shop was in fact trying to trap me in here… in either case, it occurred to me, shouting, "Hello," was hardly an appropriate response.

I stepped forward and pulled at the door knob. The door would not open. It seemed to be jammed. I hoped to goodness that it wasn't locked. I pulled at it a few times, trying the knob this way and that, but it didn't budge. For a moment I panicked, thinking that I was trapped, but then I remembered the keys. I pulled out the bundle from my pocket, and inserted the correct one into the lock. With a click, the door unlocked and swung open.

For a moment I stared at the door. How had it locked itself? It wasn't that kind of lock, you needed a key to secure it; just shutting the door wouldn't do it. I looked about me, feeling unsettled, unsure and vaguely threatened… I thought that some kind of weapon might be an idea, and grasped a pair of scissors lying on the side. With these in my hand, I stepped cautiously out of the stock room, and onto the shop floor.

The lights were all still on, the outside shutters still pulled down, the door still closed. I could see no one in the shop. On my way to the door, I looked anxiously high and low, here and there, trying to see if there was anyone in the shop, anyone hiding, perhaps hoping to rob the place. I made my way to the door, bobbing and weaving through the shop like some kind of hyperactive nervous ninja, and reached out for the door. I pulled at it. It was still locked.

I breathed a little sigh of relief and even laughed a bit. There was no one here! Of course there wasn't! It must have been a draught which pushed the door shut, and the noise which sounded like footsteps must have been something else... plenty of old buildings made weird noises. I ticked myself off mentally, and went to get my bag from behind the counter. However much I assured myself that this had all been a silly misunderstanding, a trick of my mind, I wasn't keen to stay here on my own much longer. I felt spooked, and wanted to get out into the high street, get on a bus home, and forget all this in the pleasures of a hot bath full of salts and bubbles. I shook my head and went to walk to the counter to get my bag. I put down the scissors, sliding them into a drawer on the back of the counter.

As I leaned down and reached for my bag, I stopped again. There was that sound again; tapping, as though shoes were walking over wood. I stood up rapidly from the counter and found myself staring straight into the bright blue eyes of a man with a huge red face and a short bushy grey beard leaning over the counter and glaring balefully at me. I shrieked. My bag flew out before me, falling down behind the counter, and I stumbled backwards, flailing at the man with my hands.

"Late!" he bawled at me, bashing his fists on the counter as he roared, his jowls wobbling. "Late *again*, Martha? How am I supposed to run a business with an assistant who never shows up on time?"

I fell backwards into the chair behind the counter and let it take me, stunned and terrified, travelling backwards on its little wheels across the floor. The chair made a strange little squeaking noise as it travelled which seemed incongruous against the thrill of panic thumping through my blood. My heart was loud and brash in my ears, racing at a million times a minute, but I seemed to have frozen with fear, sitting in the chair, staring at the man.

"What do you want?" I croaked. "You can take the money... just don't hurt me..."

"Get *up*, Martha!" shouted the man, turning and striding through the shop, his hands waving about. "The stock is in a mess, as always! You didn't put away the last orders properly did you? Why I keep you on is a mystery to me... what's the good of having an assistant if they don't do anything properly?"

I stared at him, wondering what on earth he was talking about. Was this some other manager I was unaware of? And why was he calling me Martha?

"My name is Hayley," I said, starting to rise from the chair, "I think there has been a mistake... sir, I think..."

I didn't get to finish. He swept back towards me, his red face almost purple as he towered over me. I cried out in alarm and ran backwards, pushing the chair between us. I pushed it out and the little chair ran on its little wheels.... And passed right through the figure of the angry, advancing man stomping towards me.

It went right through him. The thought took a little while to reach my mind as I stared dumbly at him. And now that I was staring at him, I realised I could see parts of the store... the selection of glittery Christmas party dresses, the display of scented candles... I could see them, *through him*.

That was enough for me. I turned and ran, ran for the back room, pushing the door to and locking it with shaking hands. I stepped backwards from the stock room door, pushing my back against at wall. My hands were shaking. I felt sick, and my thoughts were whirling about in my head as though they were leaves caught in the breeze. Who was this man? How had that chair passed right through him? Was he a *ghost*? What did he want?

"More to the point, Hayley," I whispered to myself, "how are you getting out of here?"

"Wanting to leave… before you've even started?" came a roar from the side of me. I leapt to my feet with a scream and turned to see the red-faced man marching through the stock room from the shadows of the back; his blue eyes were fixed on me and he was shaking his head as though bitterly disappointed. "Isn't that just like you, Martha?" he bellowed, "always shifting your way out of work, always trying to dodge your responsibilities! Well, no more of it!" He pointed wildly about him. "You will stay here and sort this mess out, and no moaning! And you'll be docked one day's pay for arriving late!"

He walked to the door, shaking his head, saying "don't know why I bother, don't know why I bother at all. Useless staff! Might as well run the whole store myself, at least then I'd know that someone could do the work properly!" and with that, he walked right through the door, disappearing from sight.

I staggered backwards and put a hand to my heart. It was racing so wildly that I thought it might conk out. My hands were shaking and my head felt strangely light, as though I might pass out. I put my hands to the sideboard and tried to steady myself. "You are not going to pass out," I whispered, "you are going to get yourself out of here…"

I thought for a moment, what could I do? My mobile! I could ring someone… *like who? Ghostbusters?* I thought, and then shook my head. I could call Kate… or Chris… someone to come and get me out of here… but getting to my phone meant going out there, with him. I had no wish to do that. But what was the alternative? Stay in here all night?

I thought about it more. If I went out there, I didn't want to stop. If I went out there then it had to be to make a run for it, and get out of the shop. My mobile, wallet and house keys were all in my purse, but I could walk home, and my neighbour had a key to let me in... However tempting the idea of getting my mobile was, I didn't want to stop for a moment. I wanted out.

I nodded to myself, yes... I would make a run for the door. I had the keys... I could make it if I just ran. After all, what was he going to do to me? Ghosts couldn't hurt people, could they? I tried to remember every ghost story I'd ever been told, and managed to freak myself out even more with half-remembered stories of headless ladies and mad-men with heads on a spike on the roof of a car... wait... had that been a ghost story?

I shook myself. This was hardly the time to try to work that out. I needed to be sharp and focussed if I was going to get out. This ghost, whoever he was, was clearly not only dead, but nuts too... and this poor Martha, this person he thought I was... Did I feel sorry for her! What a boss to have! This guy was clearly highly strung and obsessed about his store, which might also explain why he couldn't seem to leave it... even in death...

I swallowed hard and took the keys in my hands. Flicking through them, I found the one to the shop door, and the one to the shutters. I would have to work fast to get the first one undone, and then the second, and get them both shut before he came after me... but I thought I could do it. I *had* to do it! I couldn't stay in here with him! I held both the keys I needed in my sweaty palm, took a deep breath, and quietly opened the door to the shop.

It was like before. I could see no one. I could hear no footsteps, and no shouting. I couldn't see him. I stepped through and thought for a moment about going for my bag, but then thought better of it. I could get anything I left here tomorrow. For now, I needed to get out of here.

I crept across the edge of the store, past the display of novelty Christmas lights which winked and twinkled at me eerily as I passed them. I twisted my head this way and that, trying to see where he was, trying to see if I could see him. But I saw nothing. I dodged the spangley Christmas dresses, stole past the pungent glittery bath bombs, skulked around the wall of shawls and inched to the door. A long, shuddering sigh came out of me as I slid the key quietly into the lock and started to turn it.

"*Martha*!" shrieked the voice, right in my ear, causing me to jump about a mile in the air. The keys flew out of my hands and skittered across the floor, landing under a display of heavy winter coats. I let out a cry of dismay and ran after them, with the stomping steps of the ghostly manager coming right behind me. "What are you doing, girl? Trying to sneak out for lunch again, were we?"

I ignored the crazed phantom behind me and ran for the keys, dropping and sliding on my knees along the smooth wood-effect floor and grasping desperately for them under the heavy fabric of the coats. I almost had them, reaching and stretching, I could feel my fingertips touching them. I ducked down and reached for them, and then I felt a hand grasp the back of my shirt, and a strong arm pull me upright, turning me to face him. I stared at the red, almost purple, face in front of me and shrank backwards as he shook me, spitting his words into my face and screaming at me.

"Lunch can be had at your desk, Martha!" he shouted, pushing me around and marching me back to the stock room. "You don't need a break! Breaks steal money from my pocket! Eat at your counter, as you do your work! A much more efficient use of your time!" And then he pushed me into the stock room.

I staggered a few paces into the room, and looked around. The door was not closed this time, but open, and the red-faced ex-manager of the store stood there, his bright blue eyes fixed on me and his cheeks wobbling as he muttered to himself.

"I'll have to oversee you working," he cried at me, placing his hands on his hips and shaking his head. "If you can't be trusted to do it yourself. I'll have to watch you! Another fine waste of my time!"

I stared at him, feeling oddly blank and a little numb. To be honest, I think I was in shock. I didn't really know what was going on anymore, and I was quite terrified out of my wits. He had *touched* me... shoved me... pushed me... did that mean that he could hurt me? Did that mean that he could perhaps... kill me? I shivered over and over with fear, staring at him.

"Well?" he shouted, taking his hands from his hips and pointing at the boxes of goods in the stock room, "sort out this mess, Martha, and you're not leaving this store until it's all done! Moan and complain all you like, but Old Man Symmonds will teach you a thing or two about work... and about life! You don't get anywhere in life unless you're willing to work for it! Yes sir, that's the way I raised this business up out of nothing!"

He stood in the doorway, staring at me. I couldn't see a way out, and I couldn't seem to really think anymore. Mechanically, dully, with my hands shaking and my skin crawling, I turned to the boxes, and I started to sort them, glancing backwards at the glowering figure of the phantom manager in the doorway as I did so. I worked on and on, for hours. Outside, in the high street, the street lamps came on and on I worked. Gangs of people out for a drink walked past the shop doors laughing, and on I worked. Lights went out in all the other stores along the high street, people went home, and on I worked. I worked until my eyes were bleary and painful, and my back ached. But each time I thought about sitting down, I looked around to see the ghost of Old Man Symmonds staring at me, and each time it jolted my senses back into wakeful fear. I worked through the night, sorting, cleaning and arranging, until that stock room was the most ordered stock cupboard in the world.

When I put the last of the cardboard in the pile for recycling, I turned to the doorway to see the first grey lights of the dawn appearing through the little gaps in the shutters. And then I noticed that he was gone.

I had no idea how long the ghostly manager had been gone for, and at that moment, I didn't care. I sank into a little heap on the floor of the stock room, put my head in my lap, and started to cry. I was there for quite some time I think. Eventually, I got up and walked warily into the store. I walked around it for a while, trying to see if he had really gone. Although it seemed like before, when the shop floor would appear empty and then he would jump out at me, I knew, somehow, that it was not like before. He was gone. Perhaps it was the coming of the dawn, or perhaps it was the fact that I had finished the work he set me, I didn't know which, all I knew was that the very worst boss in all the world was finally gone. I sat down in the chair behind the counter, and stared at nothing, trying to make sense of all that I had seen and heard that long, long night.

As I sat on the chair next to the till, still somewhat dazed, Kate came in, pulling up the shutters and opening the door for business as usual. She stopped short when she saw me; sitting there in the clothes I had worn the day before, and stared at me.

"Have you been here… all night?" she asked with a kind of croak in her voice.

I nodded, dumbly.

She sighed and walked towards me. "So…" she said, "you met Symmonds, then?"

I nodded again. "He wouldn't let me out," I felt close to tears again.

"I'm so sorry, Hayley," she sighed, putting her bag down. "I thought that you'd be well out of here before he made an appearance. I said to be gone by seven."

I shook my head, "I lost track of time," I said, "but the stock room is very tidy now, Kate... he was quite insistent on it," and I then burst into tears again. Kate put her arms around me, and I cried into the padded shoulder of my boss without embarrassment. It took me a while to calm down, but when I did, she was looking at me kindly.

"Look, Hayley," she said, drawing a chair to sit opposite me, "I'm really sorry for everything that happened to you last night, and I'll understand if you want to leave, of course I will. But you seem like you might be a good employee, and I can't ignore that. I know this is only a stop-gap thing for you, something to bring in the money whilst you look for other things, but I could really use your help. You're good in the store, and you're useful. You're polite and helpful. I know it's not a great incentive to stay, but I could really do with someone like you around, and I promise, I'll never ask you to work late, ever again." She smiled at me and I nodded a little, she looked surprised. "You'll stay?" she asked.

"I need the money," I hiccupped. "And as long as I don't have to stay late, ever again..."

"Cross my heart," she smiled warmly. "You go home for today, and come back in tomorrow. And when you do, I'd like to talk to you about a position doing our accounts." She smiled at my surprised face, "I know that you are doing your AAT soon," she continued, "and if you wanted to go and be an accountant, I wouldn't blame you, the money is good. But if you were willing to think about it, there could be a position here for you... a bit in the store, a bit in the office, and you'd be a senior on the staff... if you'd think about it?"

I nodded. Actually, despite my dazed feelings and lack of sleep, I quite liked the idea. I took myself home and let myself in. I went to bed and fell asleep on top of the covers, in all my clothes. I slept like the dead for hours and then got up and had a long shower. It all felt like a dream, but I knew it hadn't been. Chris arrived back from his friend's house later in the afternoon, and when I told him what had happened, well… amazed isn't a big enough word to describe it…

I didn't ask him to believe me. I knew what had happened well enough. I think he was a bit worried that the whole episode might have erupted from the stress I had been under lately, but he was supportive, and didn't show too strongly that he thought it might all be in my mind. I went back to work in the shop, and found Kate to be an understanding boss. I didn't really like going into the back room, but it was so well sorted now that I didn't really have reason to… still, on the rare occasion I did go back there, I tended to try to get in and out as fast as possible, racing past the girls checking their Twitter accounts who stared at me with amazed faces at my speedy dedication to sales… if only they knew…

It was a few weeks later, after Christmas was over, when I was walking to the bus stop after my first day on the AAT course. It had gone well, and I was happy. My tutor thought as I did, that I knew basically everything I needed to know for the course, and the course itself was a formality, and a bit of rounding off to my skills. I felt as though I had new purpose in life, as though I had a plan… and even thinking of my next shift at the shop didn't seem too onerous to me now. I was still undecided about what I might do once the course was finished. Kate had offered me a job, and the money was good… but I didn't know if I wanted it, or if I wanted to go on and be an accountant instead. At this particular moment though, that didn't matter so much. I had options, and they were good. I could make up my mind about what I wanted to do once the course was done.

My mood was light and I was bouncing down the high street in my rather stylish and affordable charity-shop-bought boots when I came around a corner and almost collided with Martin, from my old work. We laughed, said hello, and caught up a little after we got over the experience of almost knocking each other flying, and he seemed really pleased to hear that I was doing so well.

"What about you?" I asked, "still slaving under Carol?"

He shook his head and laughed. "No," he said. "I went for another job at another firm, doing basically the same thing, but not working for a total loon..." He shook his head and continued, "after you left, you wouldn't believe it, she went around making out like the two of you had been the best of friends, complaining that the rest of us weren't up to the same standards, and moaning about how you'd gone because you'd been 'head hunted' as she suspected by another firm!" He shook his head again and laughed. "The woman lives in a permanent state of delusion. We're well out of that... she really was the worst boss, ever."

"Oh, I don't know," I said with a laugh. "Perhaps not the *very* worst, but she is certainly a contender for second place..."

The Christmas Ghosts

It was a dream job for me, that Christmas. The position of a house-sitter can be precarious; finding enough work to pay the bills often takes precedence over finding a nice place to stay for a week or two whilst people are on holidays, but with this one, I thought, *I've got it made*.

It was a lovely Victorian gothic cottage near to the Cornish coast, although how something this large could be described as a "cottage" was beyond me; a rambling pile of five rooms in the attics, another eight on the second storey, a huge slate-floored kitchen, tastefully restored, a parlour, master's study and other rooms on the bottom floor… if this was a cottage, then I was a small raspberry trifle.

The owners were going away for a month at Christmas to visit with family in Australia. The thought of spending Christmas in Australia was beyond me; barbecues on the beach and hot, bright sunshine just did not fit in with my ideal of Christmas. I longed for snow, every year and with no hope of that dream coming true… snow like the scenes on Dickensian Christmas cards, and a house just like the one I had now promised to sit over Christmas. And, even better yet, the house was close enough to my mother's home, about twenty miles away, so that I could spend Christmas Day itself with my family, and still take care of all my duties at work. The family I was house-sitting for seemed quite pleased, eager in fact, for me to spend Christmas Day itself with my family, and the night before. A little strange, I thought, since most house-sitting posts over Christmas generally expect you to be there all the time. But I put their happiness over my tentatively-put plans to exit their house and spend time with my own family, down to genial goodwill.

"Oh no," said Bunny, (what a name!) the mistress of the house, "we'd be more than pleased for you to go and visit your family over Christmas Eve and Christmas Day… it is *Christmas*, after all, one should be with one's family." She had that kind of accent which I generally took to be the result of years of public school, a sort-of Queenie accent, as though any moment she might descend into gags from *Blackadder*. I smiled and assured her that I would be back on Boxing Day to resume my duties at the house, and she seemed quite pleased with that.

"There are only menial duties, really," Bunny said, taking me around the house, through the lovely rooms with their open panelling and dark, oaken beams. "… Dusting, polishing; that kind of thing. Really, we just want someone here to keep the place ticking over."

"It's such a lovely house," I said appreciatively, and meant it. Although it often helps in my job to flatter a potential client's house, I really didn't have to try to fake enthusiasm with this one. It was a gorgeous house; built in 1850, retaining many original features and all its dark, moody, Victorian charm. The rooms downstairs were generous and pretty, the bedrooms, (as always with Victorian places where the rooms for entertaining were always larger) were smaller and very comfortable. There were open fires in most of the rooms and I was looking forward to using the one below in the parlour, where there was also a generous supply of seasoned logs laid in. "It will be such a pleasure… really I'm surprised you'd want to go away… I think this would make a great place to have a traditional Christmas."

"Yes…" she said, and a strange look passed over her eyes. Like a shadow, it floated across her pupils and then was gone, and she smiled at me again. "But we do so want to see George and the children. It's one of the curses of family going to live elsewhere in the world… you only get to see the grandchildren infrequently, even though we Skype and do other things like that, it's not quite the same as really seeing them." She smiled at me again. She seemed to be one of those women with an almost permanent smile on their faces, but for all her little affectations, I rather liked Bunny.

"You have excellent references," she went on, "and Talbot spoke so highly of you."

"Oh, I love looking after The Lawns," I nodded, speaking of a house which I house-sat at least once a year as its rather affluent owners jetted off to many and various exotic locations, allowing me to come into their house and basically just take management of their existing staff for several weeks a year. "Talbot and Jenny are almost like family now. I must have sat for them a hundred times over the years."

"Well, we don't have a staff like them," Bunny warned, "so there will be some cleaning required."

"That doesn't worry me in the slightest," I nodded, "in fact I am glad of a little housework, something to do on wet afternoons."

Bunny looked pleased, and went on to show me the rest of the house. It was a pleasure to think of having this place all to myself when the family was gone. The house itself was glorious, and the gardens stretched to over an acre of chiselled pathways, manicured lawns, looming clumps of heavy rhododendrons and access to a rambling route to the Cornish coastal path through one of the bottom gates. I was already planning how I would spend my time here; walking, cleaning, reading, and working on the novel I had been planning out and tentatively writing for the past year. I had gone into house-sitting in order to make money in the summer as I studied at university, and then found I liked the job so much that I just carried on. But the real dream, and one that I thought was infinitely possible seeing as my job afforded me a lot of spare time, was to write.

Oh, how I wanted to write! How I longed one day to wander into a library, look through an index and find my own name on a title of a book. The only trouble was for a long time, that I didn't really know *what* to write. I had ideas, and wrote them down diligently, then could not get any further with them. I planned out dialogue, which I then filed away, embarrassed, under piles of other papers, feeling like everything I wrote was hammy and fake. I thought about writing historical novels, and then got put off by the amount of research I seemed to need to do... for a long time, as I house-sat for the adequately rich and somewhat well-off, I thought and I thought about the fabled book I wanted to write, and fell at every hurdle. But this time, *this time*, I actually had an idea that I thought might work. I could see the characters in my mind, and I could feel them beside me as I wrote. I had started on chapters, flitting here and there in the plot as the mood took me, something I had never done before, but it seemed to work as the story flowed out with ease. When that feeling was the strongest, it was as though I was not even there anymore, as though the characters themselves were plotting and moving the story, changing it in ways that I had not planned or foreseen. In many ways, when it was going best, it was as though I was just fingers on a keyboard, recording something that was playing out in front of me.

It felt like it was going well, and although the book was by no means perfect, I was happy that the bare bones, the *heart*, of the story seemed to be coming together. I was quite excited actually; getting another position, one so remote and secluded as this house was, would enable me to really get my head down and concentrate on the story. I would have ample time to rise, do a few hours of writing, then take care of the duties in the house, polishing off each day with a ramble in the woods to refresh my mind and think over new ideas. What heaven! And as for Christmas Eve itself, and Christmas Day, I could actually spend them with the family, as my mother had been nagging me to for years. My job had largely meant that holidays were spent in the houses of other people, including Christmas, but with this position, I seemed to have fallen into an ideal situation to appease my mother and satisfy myself.

My mother's house was about twenty miles away from here, in a small town near to the coast. She and my father divorced when I was little more than a baby, and so I never knew them together as a couple. My brother said I was fortunate in this, as he, being ten years older than me, had seen all the rows which occurred in the years before they split.

"They were a nightmare together, Eloise," he sighed, shaking his head at me when I asked him about that time. "You think they're bad when they're apart? You should see them when they were together... Nitro and Glycerine... they're better off nowhere near each other."

I wondered on that at the time, I think I was about seventeen when I had asked my twenty-seven year old big brother about our parents. So much more grown up than me, at any stage of life, Simon was a lawyer with a position in a good firm, pulling in a salary which made my earnings look like a single petal in a meadow of wildflowers. He was also married, with one child and another on the way, something which gave fuel to my mother's complaints that I too needed to grow up, find a *proper* job, settle down, get married and have kids... All things I did not want to do. The divorce had made our mother into a bitter woman. She had another partner now, a man she had been with for perhaps five years, but they never seemed happy either, or at least, *she* never seemed happy. Mother was one of those people who always found something to be unhappy about, she refused to see the brighter side of anything, and would never re-fill that old, half-empty glass. She compared her life to those of other people and always found it came up short. She complained almost constantly, about anything, and seemed to take my lifestyle and my ambitions in life as some kind of personal insult. But still, she was my mother, and after years of not spending Christmas with my family, I was finally about to... just the Eve and the Day, however... any more than that and I might find the whole family thing rather too taxing.

My father had disappeared to Spain shortly after the divorce, and was living a brilliant cliché there, shacked up with his ex-secretary, who had been one of the principal reasons for my parents' split. They ran a bar together; one of those places in the south, which sell all-day English breakfasts and have *Only Fools and Horses* on perpetual re-run on the TV over the bar. He seemed happy enough, and completely unfazed about what he had abandoned over here in misty Cornwall. My brother disowned him after the divorce, and never spoke to him, but I had a kind-of contact with the father I barely remembered and hardly knew; we emailed every now and then after he contacted me through a solicitor some years back. It was only a surface acquaintance really; he was more like some kind of rakish uncle than a father.

I held no real hard feelings about growing up without a father. My mother, for all her faults, and they were many, was not a bad mother. She ensured that I was clothed, fed, educated and looked after. She was usually kind when I was small, and back then had seemed to view me and her as a kind of double-team; the last survivors of her marriage to my father. But over the years, the bitterness about her life, and the way it had turned out, seemed to overtake her. It was true that when she became a single parent she had had to give up a lot, make sacrifices for me. When I grew up she took jobs which paid the bills but didn't do much else apart from wear down her self-esteem.

"All they offer you when you've had kids is rubbish," she would say wearily when coming back after another interview, "it's like they think you've just been on holiday for ten years, rather than raising children, as if that's not a full-time job!" I sympathised, but what could I do? I couldn't offer my mother a better job, nor turn back the clock to stop her and my father having a child to "hold the marriage together" as they had thought it might... what a foolish idea! As though adding more stress and work to a relationship would hold it together when it could not survive in times of calm and peace...

She had made sacrifices, and she raised me as best she could. We weren't well-off when I was a kid, but it is a testament to her that I never noticed. It was only when I got older, and when my choice of career path became apparent, that things got sticky between us.

"A house-sitter?" she asked when I first told her of the job when I was still t university, "what does a house need sitting for?"

"People like to know that their stuff will be safe when they are away," I said, buttering my toast at the table. I was eighteen and home for summer break, about to start my first position as a house-sitter, and feeling awfully grown-up about the whole thing. "It's the best way to make sure that the place doesn't get robbed, and the money's good… it will help to pay for my half of the rent and my fees next term."

She looked at me with dubious eyes, but seemed to approve of it as a summer job. It was when I continued to do it after university that she became more and more disapproving.

"Why did I spend all that money sending you to university, if all you're going to do is sit on your arse in another person's house?" she shouted at me down the phone when I informed her I was continuing with the job when I left university.

"I paid *half* the fees, *Mother*," I said in that tone of voice which children use to their parents, and is always guaranteed to start a fight, at any age. "There isn't a lot of work out there, even for graduates… this pays well and I already have a lot of references from other jobs."

"Your brother has a good job."

I sighed down the phone. Here we go again. *Your* Brother. *Your* Brother's job. Why can't you be more like *Your* Brother? Your Brother has a job. Your Brother makes money… it was as though it was a royal title, accorded to Simon by royalty... *Your* Brother....

"I didn't train to be a lawyer, Mother, and that's not the kind of life that I want anyway..."

"What kind of life? Steady job? Good pay? Settled family life?"

The list went on and on. Eventually I put down the phone. I doubt that she noticed that I was not there anymore.

Simon always laughed when I told him that our mother held him up as the paragon of all worldly virtues for me to aspire to. "You wouldn't want my job, El," he laughed, smoothing down the front of his shirt, "it's too confining for someone like you. To be honest, I envy you at times. I make more money to be sure, but you always seem happier."

"I like what I do," I said, the words coming out defensively, even though my brother was not the one attacking me. "It pays well enough, I have my own flat, and it pays the bills... and it leaves me free to do other things."

"How's the old novel coming along?" he asked.

"Oh, you know, it takes time... research and stuff..." I said breezily, whilst inside me a different voice taunted me with all the times that I had just sat there, staring at a computer screen, unable to think what I should be writing, or all the times I had done just about anything to avoid writing, for fear of starting.

"Well, I'm sure it's a complicated process," he said, "actually, I had a few ideas... I should tell you about them one day... think it would make a great book."

Although I loved my brother, whenever people said things like that to me I wanted to scream. It's like when people say that writing must be easy, or give you a lot of time off... or when they go on and on about a friend who is a writer, "oh, so prolific! On their, what was it, Geoff? Fourth novel by now? Amazing. Just got snapped up by the agents and publishers on the first book, such a success…" They have no idea how irritating all that is… first of all, *hooray* for someone else being a fantastic success, but that's rather like pointing out to a runner how many people are ahead of them in the race… and secondly, everyone who doesn't write seems to think it's easy-peasy… that a writer sits down and bashes out a best-seller, or a Man Booker Prize winner, first time, all perfect, in their quiet and secluded study. Sorry, but no. It's not easy, especially when, like me, you can't seem to get the bloody words to come out of your head, and it's not ever, never ever, not once, for no one, perfect, first time.

I didn't even want to write a best-seller, not really. Of course the money would be nice if that somehow happened by accident, but that wasn't the point really. I just wanted to write something which would reach someone, touch them, *connect* to them. It didn't have to be everyone, just someone. I wanted to write more for me than anything else; to get out the things in my head, and see if they made sense to anyone else. I could continue happily with my day-job to bring in money to survive, and my day-job could allow me to write… as long as I could get the damn words out of my head.

But, much as we all would like to say the things which occur to us when people are irritating, we can't. So I smiled and nodded to my brother, as I smiled and nodded to everyone who said the same things to me about writing each time I admitted, (whenever I did admit, with caution and with some embarrassment) that I was a writer. I said how interesting their ideas were, and made a few vague comments about being a writer, and then dropped the subject. No one really wants to hear about your real life anyway… they like the ideal they have in their heads, which is why they are all so absolutely sure that they understand the process of writing better than you, the person actually doing it.

It's even worse when they hear you are unpublished... that is the real killer. You have to be humble, and do the tilted head, and soft, humble smile pose, when you admit that you are unrepresented and unpublished, because then everyone believes that you are just the amateur, not the professional, and you may never break into the 'proper' world of publishing and literature.

But I was determined to get there one day. I just needed a book in order to get there.

So, a month, a pay-packet, a Christmas break, time with the family, and a house in which inspiration should come just pouring from the Victorian beams, strange green wallpaper and dramatic countryside should be just the ticket, or so I thought...

I came to the house the day after the family left, collected the keys from the nearest neighbour, a good half a mile away down some twisty and high-hedged roads where ferns and brambles whipped about in the December rain and wind, and came to the front door, a rather imposing door as doors go. I turned the key in the lock and let myself into the quiet house, hearing my own footsteps echo about the walls and rooms. Putting my coat and bags down in the porch, I took a little tour of the house, finding many of the rooms closed up with the curtains drawn and a neat folder of instructions on the generous and heavy wooden table in the kitchen. Bunny had left a list of duties which she had typed out on her computer, all neatly bullet-pointed and arranged in order of the rooms. Rather nicely, the family had also stocked up the freezer with frozen meals and bread, in case I should run short, and filled the fridge with long-life milk and vegetables. I had my own car, so getting to the village shop a mile or two away would not be an issue, but it was nice to discover such treats already laid in for me, and it meant I could spend a couple of days at least in the house without having to go to the shops; a nice amount of time to get acquainted with my new charge. I found an old Edwardian desk in the corner of the downstairs parlour that afforded a spectacular view over the grounds, which sloped downhill meeting forests and the coastal path at the bottom, and decided this would be a good place to position my laptop to write.

I had already been shown the guest bedroom, which was quite large and airy, and had a handy little sink in it. The sheets had been changed and the bedspread pulled back as though welcoming me. Another nice touch… if Bunny ever needed a new profession then she would have made a great B&B owner, I thought. All that was missing was a little chocolate on the pillow…

I walked from room to room, getting familiar with the house and getting more and more pleased with myself as I wandered. Some people might have found the grand old house, with its imposing, empty rooms spooky, but I was quite at home with my own company. I never seemed to get lonely, even having done this job for so long. I was twenty-five now, and although I had had boyfriends they had never really seemed to stick. Perhaps it was my own comfort in being so at home with my own self that didn't allow for other people to enter my life with ease. I was young, I suppose, to be stuck in my ways in such a manner, but we are what we are… I think it's better to accept that, and get on with life, rather than wonder about what others have, and how they are living, as my mother always seemed to. As if her comparisons ever made her happy anyway…

I settled into a happy and easy routine in the first week. The Christmas holiday was in the third week of my post here, so I had plenty of time to myself before I had to face the onslaught of my mother and all her complaints. It pleased me to think of all the time I had ahead of me, but I didn't intend to waste any of it. I rose early, usually in the dark, since it was winter. I would come downstairs before the birds even thought to try singing, make a big pot of coffee and sit at my desk, typing away. My previous issues with the fabled writer's block seemed to have disappeared, and I figured that it was having a story, and characters that all seemed so enthusiastic in sharing themselves with me which made all the difference. Each day I wrote for several hours under the influence of a great deal of rather strong coffee, then I would do a little yoga from a beginner's guide I had on DVD and eat breakfast at the huge table in the kitchen. I then took on a few rooms of the house, figuring that rather than doing them all each day, doing a routine of deep cleaning would impress my employers more when they returned, and in my profession, having good recommendations is what it's all about.

When I was done cleaning for the day, I took myself out. Down through the gardens, a good waterproof jacket and hiking boots on, I wound my way through the wet and slippery paths, through the shadowed bushes of waxy-leaved rhododendrons, and onto the coastal path. The air was fresh and wild as it came blustering in off the sea below me, and the bark and the few remaining leaves on the trees and bushes glimmered and shone. Far below me the waves crashed frothy and white on the pebbled beaches, and out at sea I occasionally saw boats heading through the far waters. I hardly ever saw anyone else on my early-afternoon walks; the occasional jogger or dog walker, but aside from them, I was alone with the coast and its path. It was glorious.

I would get back with flushed cheeks from the wind and soggy wet hair, make myself a sandwich and a huge cup of tea, and usually settle down, eat and sometimes have a nap after lunch. Then I would get up and continue writing, or sometimes read for the afternoon, depending on how I felt. My book grew and grew, and I was feeling more and more positive about it. I would not allow myself to edit it, or go over sections as I had done in the past, often getting discouraged and displeased with my efforts as I did so... no, this time I was going to bash it all out, get it all out, and then I would go back to it as a whole to edit. And so far, this approach seemed to be working.

I spent three weeks like this, with only occasional visits to the village shop to break my schedule. The house was sparklingly clean, and I had even had a go at the gardens, keeping stray weeds from entering the paths, and clearing branches and debris which fell during storms. I was sure that Bunny was going to be happy with my efforts for her house, and I was equally sure that my own time had been well-spent in this house; the book was going well.

Then the third week came, and I started to have feelings of trepidation about finally getting to spend a Christmas with my family. Simon and his wife Kira would be there, with their son, Noah, and I was looking forward to seeing them, but it was my mother who I was dreading. The thought made me feel guilty, as per usual, which only added to the sense of dread at the coming holiday. But as the day got closer I shook myself. "It's two days," I said aloud, my voice sounding small inside the empty house, "just two days, stop being such a baby, you can do this. Just smile and nod, ignore her criticism, and get on with it. Then you have another week here with the book before the family come home."

Another week, that was all. I felt quite sad. It wasn't just that this house was gorgeous, and a pleasure to be in. The house had helped me in some way that all the others I had sat had not. The seclusion, the peace, the situation... all of them had helped me to actually get the words out of my head and on to paper... and some of it was really quite good, I hoped. I didn't want to leave, I wanted to stay... I wanted for this to be *my* house.

"One day," I said, mocking myself with a grin in the mirror as I looked myself over, ready to take a small bag of my clothes and a larger one of presents to my mother's house, "when the novel becomes a best-seller, then you can *buy* this house." I smiled at my own mocking tone and shook my head. "Right, Eloise, shoulders back, smile on, and get on with it. Two days will be done and dusted in no time."

It was the morning of Christmas Eve, and I was packed and ready to go. I took one more look in the mirror, and then went to the front door, but as I turned myself out of the door and set my bag down, fishing about for the key in my pocket, I heard a noise. I stopped for a moment, stopped my hands moving about in my pocket, and listened. There it was again, I was sure I had heard it now… a noise like footsteps… somewhere inside the house.

I froze at the door for a moment, trying to hear it again, but could not. Then, as I was standing there, I heard another noise. It seemed to come from a room to the left of where I stood at the front door; from the parlour, my own writing room. I thought for a moment. I was sure that all the doors and windows were secured. I had only just checked them all over as I was to leave the house that morning. Could someone have managed to get into the house?

I listened again; there it was, a noise like footsteps… deep within the house, and a rustling noise coming from closer by, like the swish of long skirts… for a moment I thought about calling the police then and there. Little hairs were standing to attention all over my body, and I felt a chill spreading over me which had nothing to do with the cold December air. I pushed the door open, and it creaked loudly, "Hello?" I called, standing at the door and feeling foolish even as I shouted, "…is anyone there?"

A little rush of cold air seemed to flow towards me, but from where I did not know, seeing as all the doors and windows were shut. It brushed through my clothing, making me shiver. I felt uneasy and unsettled; the house, *my* house, this lovely place where I had found such peace and inspiration suddenly felt alien and uncanny. I could not describe where that feeling came from, but I felt unwelcome, and out of place. I pushed the door again and stepped back into the house.

"Hello?" I called again, and my voice gave a little squeak of fear at the end of the 'o' as I spoke. I flushed, as though someone could see my silly embarrassment, and found myself telling myself off inside my head, telling me to get on with it, go see what the noise was… it was probably nothing, old houses make noises all the time…

I walked into the porch and through the archway into the parlour where I switched on the light. The room was just as I left it: the fireplace stocked with wood and a pile beside it ready to be used; the comfortable sofas with their tapestry-esque patterned fabric nestled near to the fire; the little Edwardian writing desk near to the window, where I sat to write… all normal, nothing disturbed, no one here.

I walked out of the room, looking behind me more than once with a swift frightened and fearful glance. I felt almost as though someone was here, and they were watching me… even though I knew there was no one in the room. I made a tour of all the rooms, having to take a deep breath before going into some of the darker ones. I switched on all the lights. I checked everywhere. I found nothing.

In the end I found myself back at the front door feeling a little puzzled. It had certainly sounded as though there was someone in the house, and I had not, not in the whole time I had been here, once felt uncomfortable in the house as I had done this morning. I shook my head. I was imagining things, I told myself. The house was old; plumbing, draughts, old wiring… all these things can make noises, and the brain just fills in the gaps. There had been nothing there in the first place, and I had simply managed to scare myself into thinking that there was. I shook my head and picked up my bag, pulling the heavy door to, and locking it. Then, running through the rain, I got into my car and drove the twenty miles or so to my mother's house.

The rain and wind on the journey were not pleasant to drive in. I had to keep the heaters blasting away so that I could see through the steamed-up windows, and more than once had to come to a sliding, skidding halt when I met other cars on the tiny, bendy lanes. I was feeling rather unnerved by the noises I had thought I heard in the house, and also feeling rather grateful, in a way, that I had somewhere else to go to tonight. I was sure that the noises had been nothing, but then, there was something at the back of my thoughts which kept telling me that I *had* heard something… was I neglecting my duties to my employers? I had looked through the house and found nothing, but still… I was a little worried. I assured myself that I could not call the police out on the basis that I had heard something, if I *had* heard it, and found nothing whilst doing a search of the property, they would think I was insane, but still, the worries niggled at the back of my mind as I drove.

When I eventually reached my mother's little house, seated in a nice estate near to the park and estuary in the village she lived in, I parked out front, gathered my bags and walked right into the midst of complete confusion, so it seemed. Simon opened the door and gave me a hug, and I was immediately assaulted by my four-year-old nephew Noah, who ploughed into me, only stopping because he bashed straight into my pelvis and banged his head, once on me, and then on the wall as he bounced off, causing him to immediately break into howls of distress. Simon gathered his son up and threw him almost over his shoulder, saying to me, "don't worry about it, he's going through a phase… crying and wailing like a banshee at the slightest knock." I gave Simon a smile and divested myself of my coat, coming into the kitchen and leaving my little bag in the hall. My mother was in the kitchen, surrounded by plumes of delicious smelling mist coming from the foods she was already preparing for Christmas Day.

"Hi, Mum," I said, coming over and giving her a kiss, "need any help?"

"Of *course* I need help," she said waspishly, as a warning signal went off in my head; oh dear, she was wound up already. "Everyone seems to think that I can do this all by myself," she continued, brandishing a batter-laden spoon about her. I smiled at her, washed my hands in the sink, found an apron and got to peeling vegetables; there was little, I reasoned, that she could find fault with in my peeling of vegetables.

Tom, my mother's long-term partner, walked in to take three beers from the fridge and waved one at me in offering, which I took gladly. A little alcohol might help steady my nerves from that morning, and might dull the sharpness of my mother's tongue too. Cracking them open, he set one before me.

"Doing alright?" he asked, "new place you're looking after okay?"

"Good thanks, and yes, the house is lovely. Very posh. Old Victorian house."

"Good, good," he replied with a smile, "come in and watch the film if you get tired with the veg, won't you?"

I grinned at him and nodded, I liked Tom, he was a nice guy, and seemed to take my mother's endless complaints as though they were nothing. I wondered how he put up with it, but then, perhaps my mother was only like this with me? How would I know unless I was here all the time, and invisible? My mother clucked at him. "She's got no time to be sitting on her arse like you lot," she said darkly, "Eloise is helping me with the food, it's not like it wouldn't hurt you to muck in."

"I'm helping with the child care and entertaining our other guests, my love," he said in a sweeping, breezy fashion, and then grinned and left the room, taking the beers with him.

"Other guests?" I asked.

"He means Simon and Kira," she said, speaking of my brother and his wife.

"I should go and say hi." I put down the peeler and made for the door. My mother didn't stop me, but I heard a sigh of exaggerated exasperation as I left the room. "I'll only be a mo, Mum," I shouted back to answer her sigh.

Kira was propped up on the sofa with a great belly sticking out before her and her feet up on a cushion on the little table. She smiled at me in a slightly pained way as I greeted her and patted the seat next to her. "Come keep me company, Eloise," she sighed, "all they are doing is talking football... I can't stand it."

I smiled. "Can't stay for long," I warned her, "Mum has me peeling the veg."

Kira made a face and we both laughed. I knew her opinion of our mother was that she was rather difficult. Although Kira didn't get the "Your Brother" comments, being married to Simon after all, she had gone through several rounds of the "How to Raise your Kids" lectures, of which Mum was a regular and principal speaker. Not being a blood relation, I think Kira had gone through more years than she really needed to of trying to be overly polite to mum, and taking her medicine as it was dished out to her. Now that she had borne one child to the family line and was brewing another in her belly, I think she had had enough of Mum's obsession with telling everyone else how they ought to live, raise their kids, speak, work... breathe...

"Your mum has been making the biggest fuss about dinner," she whispered to me. "Keeps telling me that it is, of course, more complex, than the dinner I made for the family last Christmas..."

"Well, of course," I grinned, "it always is, when Mum does it."

Kira shook her head, "and she's been feeding Noah nothing but sugar since first thing this morning. If I was able to catch him, I would have searched his pockets for all the sweets he's had off his nana today, but with this lump..." She put her hands over her swollen belly and sighed.

"You must be almost there now, though?" I asked. "Can't be more than a couple of weeks?"

"A week, and believe you me, El, I'm looking forward to getting this one out and getting being pregnant over and done with. It's all lies, you know? They tell you that pregnancy is a magical time; full of glowing faces and wondrous joy… it's bloody not! You get a sore back, swollen ankles, swollen fingers… swollen everything! You can't sleep, you feel sick for the first few months and look like a cow the rest of the time. I swear, God must be a man, because no woman would have invented this way of doing things."

"You get a baby at the end of it though," I said. "Hopefully that makes it worth it?"

"I love kids, El," she said darkly, "that doesn't mean I don't think that this whole bringing them into the world thing should have been shared more equally between men and women, if there was any justice in the universe, we'd be like sea horses… the women carry the babies for a bit, and then the males take over… much better."

We laughed and she patted a hand over mine. "Go on," she said, "you'd better get back before your ma skins you."

Just at that moment there was a cry from the kitchen, "Eloise Susan Appleyard… are you helping me with this dinner, or what?"

"Coming, Mother," I shouted, as I patted Kira's arm and got up. In our house, when you heard your full name, you always knew you were in trouble. "You two could be helping out too, you know?" I said to my brother and Tom who were apparently engrossed in discussion with each other about football, whilst also simultaneously watching *Finding Nemo* on TV.

"Can't neglect our guests," said Tom happily.

"You went in there and offered, El," responded Simon, grinning merrily, "you only have yourself to blame."

That was true enough. I had no defence there. I walked back into the steam, and into a slowing boiling pot of my mother's dissatisfaction with me and my life. It didn't take long to come out…

"*So*," she said, with that tone of voice that only my mother can put into "so,"… "So, will you take another house-sitting job when this one is done with?"

I nodded, carefully peeling the multi-coloured carrots which Tom grows proudly in his allotment. Orange is apparently, not the only carrot, and Tom is always glad to tell and re-tell the story of the orange carrot and its tyrannical path to world domination over the older, more varied tones of carrot colours. I concentrated on the carrots, hoping that my nod was enough of an answer. I didn't want to get into a discussion on the subject of my employment with my mother really, because no matter how innocent it sounded, it was not.

"Are you not thinking that perhaps might be the time to start training for a *real* job?" asked my mother, and something inside me seemed to chime, as though she had hit a hammer down on one of those fairground games, and hit the bell with the strength-o-meter. Ah, here it was… Ding-ding! Round one.

"I *have* a job," I replied, "and there is nothing improper about it."

"It's not a real job though, is it? Like being a baby sitter."

"Some people do that for a day job," I said mildly, "there are many professions in fact in care… caring for people, for children, for animals."

"Not for houses though," she said bluntly, angrily shaping balls of sage and onion stuffing mixed with sausage meat and starting to put them on a tray ready for the fridge overnight. "I mean, it doesn't require any *skill*, does it?"

"Don't you think that your housework requires any skill, then?" I asked, gritting my teeth and taking up the parsnips. I never liked parsnips, horrible dry things even at the best of times. It was good to be peeling a vegetable I didn't like as my mother quizzed me. I could vent my feeling on the parsnips rather than my mother.

"It requires effort, patience, and some skill I suppose," she said grudgingly, not wanting to reward me with any praise, but not wanting to disparage her own role within the house either. "But it's not like a *real* job is it? Not like it pays much. When I think of how well your brother is doing…" She trailed off with a sigh, which I matched.

"Mother, my job *is* a real job. I do work, and I am paid accordingly. I get to pay the bills, and I get to do something I like. What is wrong with that?"

Her hands dropped to the kitchen table, sending a *poof* of flour sailing into the air as she stared at me. "I gave up a lot so that you could have a good education, go to a good school, go to a good university… You got good grades, a good degree… why not actually do something with that, instead of wasting your time pottering around in empty houses and playing about with this writing?" She laughed a humourless and bitter laugh. "And what are you going to do with that when you're old? How are you going to support yourself in later life? I know that you don't save anything, you can't, on the wages you earn."

"I'm pretty young, Mum, I don't need to think about saving until later in life, and as for the writing, well, actually, and since you ask, the book is going rather well. I'm hoping it might be finished by the time I leave, as a first draft at least."

"Pah!" She gestured wildly with a sausage-covered hand, sending little flecks of pink meat flying across the kitchen. "Pie in the sky... you think it's all so easy, don't you? That you'll just write a best-seller and that will be the end of all the work you'll have to do for the rest of your life? Well let me tell you, *Missy*, life doesn't work like that. You've got to put in the hours, you've got to sweat and toil, and even then, you don't get anywhere, so..."

"So what's the point of even trying?" I snapped, my voice raised, "is that your point, Mother? Is that the point of this new and glorious lecture on my life? What's the point of trying at anything, since you won't get anywhere anyway? Then what does it matter that I work sitting houses? What does it matter if I write a book, or two, or ten? If everything is so very pointless, then why should it matter that I don't have the same ambition as Simon? That I don't want a regular, boring desk job?" I slammed the peeler down on the table and glared at her. "What you are really trying to say is that there *is* a point, as long as I do what you want me to do... what you are really trying to say is that there is no point in doing what *I* want to do, isn't that it?"

I was almost shouting now, and hadn't even noticed I was standing, facing her across the table, with my hands resting on it for support in a perfect mirror-image of her pose. She opened her mouth, and was about to say something, when Simon appeared at the kitchen door, hovering with an alarmed look on his face.

"Er... Eloise," he said, flushing, the way he always did when he was about to lie. I often wondered how on earth he managed to be a lawyer, with such a disability, but perhaps it only happened when we saw him, we did know him better than anyone else, after all. "Eloise... er... Kira wants to talk to you about something," he muttered and then walked in with a smile at Mum, "I'll help out with the veg, eh?" He picked up the peeler from where I had slammed it on the table and nodded to me, as if to say, *"get out, while you still can."*

I left. Walking into the sitting room and trying to have a normal conversation with Tom and Kira, whilst Noah zoomed around the room and my blood rumbled into a steady and uneasy simmer. Fights should not be left like that... nothing was solved between me and Mum, and had Simon not interrupted, perhaps we finally would have gotten things out in the open. But we hadn't. That came later.

That night, we settled in around the dining table to eat a rather good beef stew that Mum had made, along with steamed dumplings and rustling roast potatoes. "All I had time to do," she muttered darkly, as though anyone was going to say that it wasn't nice as we started to eat. "What with everything else I've had to do today, and this week."

"It's delicious, Susan," said Kira sweetly, starting to eat in a steady manner, but looking as though she could quite happily eat all our portions and not be full. I grinned and passed her the bread, which she took from me, putting several pieces at the side of her plate.

"You want to watch your portions in the later months of pregnancy," Mum warned, waving a fork at Kira. "It's not true, all that eating for two, you know. You'll have a hard time shifting that weight when the baby comes."

"Mum!" said Simon, watching a shade of crimson work its way up Kira's throat and cheeks; she smiled wanly at him and shook her head. *Don't start*, is what that look said. I watched Kira's embarrassment and my anger at my mother seemed to have been turned up a notch on the stove...

"So, El," said Simon, trying to smoothly cover up the latest instalment of our embarrassing mother, "how's the book going?"

I ignored a little snort from my mother, and smiled at him. "Really well, actually, Si," I said brightly, knowing my tone would annoy Mum. "This new place I'm looking after, it's been so good for the writing process... secluded, far off, no distractions. I've been getting my head down for hours each day and it's really coming on."

"Have you sent anything to publishers?" asked Kira, buttering her bread.

"No, you've got to send samples to agents first anyway," I replied. "Publishers won't take unsolicited manuscripts anymore. You have to get an agent, who likes your work or rather, who thinks they can sell your work, then they approach publishers for you..." I paused and ate a mouthful of the stew, it really was delicious. "But," I continued, "I'm thinking about self-publishing anyway."

"Why do that?" asked Tom, "*can* you do that, anyway? Don't you need a publisher to take you on?"

"Not anymore," I said, "independent publishing is the new thing. Even traditionally published authors use it from time to time. It means I get to keep creative freedom over the book, and I get seventy per cent of the royalties, whereas with traditional publishing the author only gets about fifteen at best."

"Seventy per cent of nothing, well, that's quite something isn't it?" laughed my mother. I felt the stove go up another notch. I ignored her.

"Anyway, I'll have to wait until it's done in any case," I said, "before I make a final choice."

There was another snort from my mother, and I turned to her. "What is it, Mother?" I asked.

She glared at me; she hadn't calmed down from this morning either, and was clearly still in a stink with me. "It's all pie in the sky stuff with you, always was Eloise," she spat at me, "you think life's all easy and things just fall in your lap. Well let me tell you that life isn't like that. And what's going to happen when this book dream of yours falls through, like we all know it will? What will you have to fall back on when you're old, eh? Going to house-sit for the rest of your life?"

"Even if I did choose to do that," I replied, setting down my spoon and scowling at her, feeling her negative words cut all the way through every ounce of self-confidence I had gathered in writing my book over the past few weeks. It was as though my mother was the one person in all the world who truly knew where and when to strike at me in order to strip everything from me, every bit of confidence, self-assurance, happiness… like I was roasted meat she was stripping to make a stew. And in that moment, I hated her for it. Hated her for trying to put me down. Hated her for ruining my dreams. Hated her for trying to make me as worthless as she felt, just so that she could have a companion in her misery. Oh yes, I was sure that was why she wanted to drag me down with her; to stop me from ever trying to do anything I wanted. Nothing I wanted to do was ever good enough for my mother. It had to be what *she* wanted of me… a boring life in a tidy office, a pension plan and a dull husband to come home to. She didn't understand my life, and she didn't respect it. She never would, and I decided then that I should stop trying to make her. "Even if I did choose to do that, *Mother*," I continued, "then what would be the problem? My job pays the bills and lets me do what I want. I don't live to work, I work to live. It suits me, and I'm happy. Shouldn't that be what concerns you? That your children are happy? Or do you just not recognise that emotion anymore, because it's been so long since you did anything but moan and criticize that you wouldn't know happiness if it came and slapped you round your big fat face?"

I slammed my spoon down to a resounding shocked cry of "El!" from everyone at the table apart from Noah, who sat staring at us all with round eyes, his red plastic spoon hovering half-way to his mouth, dripping beef stew on his front and on the tablecloth. I felt as thought I didn't care anymore. I was energized by my anger. I stood up and rushed from the table, wanting to put distance between my mother and me. I went out into the hallway, and saw my bag still sitting there, as though it knew that I was going to come back for it, as though it knew that I wasn't going to stay. I grabbed it and marched to the front door. I wasn't going to stay here and have my life insulted by my mother! I wasn't going to stay here and let her disintegrate any self-confidence and happiness I had... It was a mistake, coming here, thinking that I could spend a day or two with my mother without her attacking me. I would go back to the house, and get back to work. Hang Christmas! What did I care for it anyway? I had spent enough Christmas Days alone and without family, why did I need them now?

I caught a glimpse of myself as I marched to the door, and stopped, seeing this alien creature in the mirror as I passed. Her cheeks were bright with anger, and her brown eyes snapped at me in the mirror. Her jaw was set and her teeth clenched. She looked ready to take on anyone, to take on the world. That's how I felt then, I guess. I could take on anything. I didn't need anyone else. I was pulsing with the force of my anger and hurt. I was ready for a fight, with anyone, and about anything.

I had to get out of there, I thought suddenly, the thought coming like a wash of cold water over me, before I said anything else, to another member of my family, and had them enraged at me too.

I could hear noises of argument from the dining room, and as I took hold of the door and yanked it open, Simon came tumbling from the room, looking for me. "El," he said, his voice managing to be both weary and excited at the same time. "Don't go. It's *Christmas*."

"I can't stay here, Simon," I spat; talking through gritted teeth is never easy. "I can't stay in the same house as that woman. Don't you see? Nothing is ever going to change. I thought I could come here and spend a couple of days with you all, but she had to start attacking me, throwing you and all your accomplishments at me. She never stops to think what she is saying, and she never asks what I might want out of life. She just goes on and on about all the sacrifices she had to make for me when I was born, well, I'm sorry…"

My mother's face, red with anger, appeared in the door way, and she opened her mouth to say something, but I cut her off.

"Yes, I'm *sorry*, Mother," I shouted at her, "sorry that having me didn't save your terrible marriage; sorry that you had to give up all your own dreams to support me; sorry that father ran off with another woman and left you all alone and bitter. And most of all, I'm sorry that I've been such a burden to you all my life. I never turned out as you expected, and so I've let you down. Well, you won't have that problem anymore. This is the last you will see of me, I promise you. Imagine that you never had a daughter, and you might be a little happier than you can be living with a daughter who disappoints you! We're done! I want nothing more to do with you. This is my life, and I will live it as I choose to, not as you dictate!" she went to speak again and I held up a hand. "No more, Mother," I said. "We're done. I'm through with you."

Then I turned to Simon and nodded curtly at him. "Simon," I said, in that ridiculously formal manner one gets when angry, "I'll be sure to come and see you when my nephew or niece is born. Have a good Christmas."

And then I pulled the door open, and almost ran from the house, through the falling rain, past the street lamps which were shining against the darkness of the night, and into my cold car. I didn't stop to turn on the heating, or put on my seat belt. I just started the engine and drove off. I wasn't even looking which way I was going at first, and drove around the inner part of the village twice before finding the road out again, but I didn't care. I strapped on my seat belt as I drove, pulling and yanking the thing in anger so that it stuck several times as I cursed at it. I put the heating on full blast and drove too fast out into the lanes. In the distance I could hear church bells ringing, calling people to the night services for Christmas Eve, and I switched on the radio to drown out the noise. I didn't want to hear sounds of other people having a happy Christmas when I was having such a miserable one. As I drove, and thoughts of the fight with my mother stewed over in my mind, I felt like crying, but I gripped the steering wheel and let out sounds of anger instead. I was in such a temper that I hardly remembered the strange noises of the house as I had left it that morning until I reached the driveway itself.

It was only, in fact, as I pulled into the gravelled driveway and saw a light shining from a room in the attic of the house that I thought of the strange noises, and remembered my feelings of unease that morning.

I stopped the car, and stared at the house. I was sure that I had turned all the lights out when I had left. I had gone through each room, turning them off, and making sure of it, just as I had turned off the hot water advance on the boiler, and turned the house heating down to a steady temperature. I was sure I had… but yet… there was this light still burning, glowing out of the house and through the misty rain like a little torch. I shook my head and gathered the contents of my bag, pulling my hood on my coat up whilst still in the car. I must have left it on by mistake, I thought. I sighed unhappily. It was late. I was tired, I was miserable. I would go inside, turn the heating up and have a bath to soothe me before I tried to sleep. With all the thoughts rattling about in my head, I could do with a little time to wind down. Perhaps I'd watch some TV in bed, I thought. There was a TV set in my room, which I had barely used since I had been here. Preferring to spend my time writing or reading, my busy days had often expelled the need for TV. But with my mind whirring and my feelings bruised, I felt as though staring at some inane programmes might be quite welcome.

It was then that the light in the attic went out. Blink, and it was gone. I looked up at the house again, staring at it. Had the light been on at all? Was I seeing a reflected light from a ship out at sea or something? I turned myself to look in the direction of the sea out front of the house, and then whipped my head back as another light came on, in the room next to the first. I stared at it, and for a moment I was sure that I could see a dark shape moving in the room, but then there was nothing. The light still shone, but as I looked at it, it seemed to me that it was not bright enough for an electric light. It looked almost as though it was from a lamp, or a candle, there was something of that flickering element to it… electric lights are not affected by draughts after all… good grief, I thought, it's probably a burglar… someone must have broken in after all, and now they are scouting the place with a torch or a candle.

I pulled my mobile out of my bag and called 999, explaining down the fuzzy line to the lady on the other end that I was a house-sitter, that I had left the house I was sitting for a few hours, and now there seemed to be prowlers on site. My hands were shaking as I sat in my car, waiting for the police who the operator assured me would be there within ten minutes. I wondered if I should get out of the car, or drive backwards up the drive? What if there was more than one of the prowlers and they had heard or seen the car? Would I be safe, sitting here, a woman alone against however many of them there were? But then, if I drove backwards, would they hear the sound of the engine, something they might have missed before, and run off, or worse still, come looking for me?

I didn't know what to do, and the minutes went by feeling like hours, like years. My breath fogged up the windows of the car, and I had to wipe the glass over and over to be able to see. The light seemed to be moving through the rooms, and it was certainly not the electric light of the rooms themselves, I was sure of that now. I was also pretty unsure it was a torch as I had thought… that flickering, wavering quality it had… it looked like a flame to me, gas or candle, something like that. It reminded me of the Tilly lamps we used to take on camp when I was little, but why would any self-respecting burglar be using such an archaic method of lighting for his Christmas robberies? Had he lost his torch and was using the emergency supply of candles Bunny had showed me for power cuts, kept in the kitchen drawer? Perhaps that was it, perhaps the power was out… thoughts and more thoughts ran through my head and my heart seemed to quicken with each newer and more bizarre theory…

Eventually, I saw lights in the distance, and a police car zoomed down the drive, pulling up behind me. There was only room in this drive for one car at a time, so they stopped behind me and climbed out, one man and one woman. I almost leapt from the car and ran to them.

"I think it's prowlers," I said in a rush.

"You're the one who called, Miss?"

"Appleyard, and yes," I said breathlessly, feeling infinite relief that someone was here finally and I was not alone. "I'm the house-sitter; the family is out in Australia for the holidays. I went out for a few hours, and when I came back, there was a light on…. There!" I turned to the house to point, and my hand fell down slowly and gently.

The house sat peaceful and still in the darkness. All the lights were off.

I turned back to the police in some confusion, "It was just on, I tell you," I said. "There was a light, moving from room to room. Please, this place is my responsibility, I have to make sure that it and the belongings of my employers are safe."

The police man tilted his head to one side and looked at the house. Then he nodded to me. "We'll go take a look inside, Miss Appleyard, you come with us, and stand behind us, if there is someone in there, I don't want you getting hurt. Equally, I'm not leaving you out here alone if there is any danger from these people."

I hurried and stumbled behind the steady and calm steps of the police. They both seemed entirely unruffled by such an experience, whereas I, in all my inexperience, was a mass of hyper-energy, half excited by such a thing, and half wanting to go and hide in my car again.

We got to the front door, and found it locked as I had left it. I produced the key and the policeman tried to open it gently and quietly, and failed due to the ancient nature of the old door. He cursed slightly as it opened, and then pushed it open fully. The policewoman switched on a torch produced from her side and shone it through the room. Nothing moved; in the hallway, the grandfather clock started to chime out midnight, making us all jump, but there were no other sounds. The police officers moved forwards, they walked into each room on the ground floor, shining their torches and then turning on the lights. There was nothing in any of the rooms, and there was no sign that any of the windows or doors had been forced open. We moved up, through the house, and as we entered more rooms and found no sign of any person, or any disturbance, I began to feel more and more foolish, and less afraid. My cheeks started to flush with embarrassment as they went diligently through the rooms, and I joined in the search with more and more desperation, almost hoping that some villain *would* leap out from behind a curtain and attack me, rather than undergo the various glances the police were giving to each other.

We came to the end of the search, and there was nothing. They had looked in every room, behind every curtain, in every cupboard; there was no one in the house, and no sign that there ever had been.

We came downstairs and I stood in the porch, feeling miserable and foolish. "I am so sorry," I stuttered, not daring to look them in the eyes. "I… I was sure that I saw something."

"Don't you trouble yourself, Miss," said the female police officer, an older, matronly looking woman who reminded me a little of my mother, except that she was smiling gently. "Sometimes, when you're by yourself, it's easy to get spooked, especially in an old house like this. You did the right thing to call us, if it had been anything then you were doing right by your employers, and it might have been dangerous for you." She looked at me with a little concern. "Do you have anywhere else to go, tonight?" she asked, "family... or friends? Might be better to stay with someone else, and come back here with fresh eyes in the daylight." She gave a sort of half-wink. "The worries of the night are often banished by the coming of the dawn," she said, poetically, I thought, for a policewoman.

I shook my head. "I was with family," I said, "but we... well, there was a fight, and I left to come back here. I don't have anywhere else to go at short notice like this. I live in Bristol."

The policeman made a sort of comradely grimace, and nodded knowingly. "Fights are traditional at Christmas, my love, don't worry, it will all come out in the wash." He nodded to me, "perhaps that's what it was, if you don't mind me saying, Miss... perhaps you were upset by the fight, and your mind played tricks on you... the mind's a funny thing you know."

"Perhaps..." I said, wondering how on earth having a fight with my mother could transpire into seeing a light move through the house when I got back here. Suddenly I just felt tired, so very tired. I guess all the adrenalin was wearing off. "I'm so sorry to have called you out for no reason," I said. "And thank you so much for all your help... err... would you like a coffee or something?"

They both shook their heads at me. "No, but thanks," the woman said, and then passed me a card with their numbers on it, and the number of the local station. "Just in case you do see anything suspicious, give us a ring, we're on duty all night, and we can be here in no time at all." She nodded to me and smiled, saying "lock up when we're gone, and get yourself to bed."

They left, and I duly locked the front door, then walked through the house, turning on all the lights. I didn't want any shadows to spook me. Deciding to forgo the bath idea, I walked up the stairs and hurried into my room. It felt chilly everywhere, but the heating had been left on low so the house should have been warm enough. Not wanting to go and inspect the boiler right now, I pulled on thick fleece bottoms and put a jumper over my pyjamas, then climbed into bed, leaving a light on next to me. I could not sleep in the full force of the room's lights, but I didn't want to wake up in darkness. As I climbed into bed, I put a large Maglite from my bag on the pillow next to me, and after thinking for a moment, curled the heavy and reassuring weight of the torch in my hand. It seemed to reassure me enough that I fell into a deep, black sleep of nothingness through the night.

And then I awoke sharply and suddenly on Christmas morning, staring with confused horror at the shape of a young woman standing at the end of my bed, staring out of the window.

I blinked several times, and then sat up with a start, letting a strange noise out of my throat at the same time. It was low, animalistic sound, a sound of fear. The young woman was standing at the end of my bed, turned half away from me. Her hands hung at her side, and she stared out at the sea with an expression of complete hopelessness and despair. Sadness seemed to radiate from her, and I felt it hit me as I looked on her with dazed amazement.

"Who are you?" The words tumbled out of my mouth in more of a croak than anything else, and I trembled, looking on this astonishing, alien visitor standing in my room. She did not acknowledge me, nor seemed to have heard me at all. She just kept staring out of the window. A knock at the closed door of the room sent me sprawling up to the head of the bed, bringing my Maglite with me, holding it outstretched and in trembling hands. I had no idea what was going on… was this a dream? Was I still asleep? I felt quite awake enough... was this the intruder I had seen last night? And if so, why was she just standing in my room, not even looking at me?

The door opened and I scrambled back on the bed to a standing position, holding the Maglite out before me as though I was about to challenge someone to a duel. It shook in my hands and I could hear my heart beating in my ears like a drum.

"Who are you?" I cried again, my voice more sure this time even though it shook with fear. "What do you want? I'll call the police!" The girl ignored me again as the door swung open and a man stood there, staring at her and glowering at her, his face a mask of anger.

"Are you coming down to talk to Sir John?" he asked, the huge whiskers of two massive side-burns waggling on a face with heavy jowls as he spoke. "He has come especially for this day, to talk with you in earnest about his proposal."

"I have no wish to marry such a man as he," said the girl, crossing her arms before her and staring at the man in the doorway with equal anger. "Rich he may be, Father, but he is a cruel man, rude and uncouth. It is your wish I marry him, not mine!"

I stared at the two for a moment, wondering once again if I was in the middle of a dream or not. The woman was wearing a long, dark green dress, made in a most archaic style... it looked Victorian to me, although I had little experience of the clothing of such times. But the long dark dress, with a little lace at the collar and cuffs, the way her thick blonde hair was made up... yes, she looked like she had wandered straight out of one of those BBC costume productions of *Wuthering Heights* or something... and the man too... his suit and waistcoat were dark blue, and his whiskers were out of this world, and time... what on earth was going on here?

"What do you want...?" I croaked again, but hardly got any further. I was just staring at them now, utterly bemused. They did not seem at all interested in me, and if these were burglars, then they were the most bizarre kind. My heart was hammering away in my chest, but I lowered the Maglite and stood up at the side of the bed. They did not note my presence, and continued to talk in an agitated fashion about this Sir John, until the man ordered the girl out of the room and down the stairs. She hurried past him with tears in her eyes.

I felt a kind of horrid fascination which I was unable to resist, and out of the room I padded after them on bare feet, my Maglite weapon left on the covers of my bed as I hurried after the shape of the fleeing girl.

Downstairs, it was as though I had indeed wandered into a dream. There were people and movement everywhere. In every room there were servants hurrying past with plates of food and glasses of drink, the kitchen was a roar of activity with a woman dressed in a deep black dress thundering commands at each passing maid or man. In the parlour, I stood in my pyjamas, staring with an open, gaping mouth at the throng of richly dressed men and women milling about in there. The blonde girl from my room was now seated at a piano which had not been there the night before, and was playing a haunting tune, most unfitting for Christmas. Evidently I was not the only one who thought that her tune was too sad for Christmas, as her father, the one with the whiskers, barked at her to change the tune. She took up with *God Rest You Merry Gentlemen* instead, and managed to make it sound as sorrowful as the song she had played before.

I just stood there. In my pyjamas and baggy jumper. Staring at the people around me. I had no idea what was going on, and had no explanation for the whole thing other than to think I was indeed still asleep. It was all too fantastic for words. I could even smell the scents of cooking food from the kitchen, the scent of gas lamps placed in the darker rooms, the smell of the people, their sweat, the wine in their glasses...

I just stood and stared. In all honesty, I think I was what is known as dumb-struck.

I followed people about here and there. No one seemed to see me. It was as though I was a ghost, and then I thought to myself, somewhere in the tumbling confusion of my mind... it is *not you*, who is the ghost...

The thought made my skin tremble with fear, but yet, it seemed that I had nothing to fear... was this, then, what had caused me to see lights in the house last night? Was this, then, why Bunny and co. had been so keen to have me out of the house on Christmas Day? Could it be that this odd little happening was not unexpected? Was this why the family went away at Christmas? It all seemed to be adding up, and making a sum of I did not know what... but I was fascinated. I wandered through the party of rich people, listening to their conversations. There was something almost heady about the experience, as though I was the invisible woman. What a strange power to have! Most of the conversation was of nothing; the state of the roads, how the Queen would be spending Christmas at Balmoral (I had to remind myself, that this was Queen Victoria they were speaking of), the wonders of an exhibition they had attended... all rather trifling conversation, and yet to me, this unseen observer in this strange land, it was fascinating, and wonderful.

When one of the guests stepped backwards and walked straight through me I felt a sudden shiver, almost of pain, and vowed not to let that happen again. It was a most unpleasant feeling, and reminded me with a tremor of the uncanny, that I was wandering through a ghost story.

And then I heard someone talking of something which seemed to catch my ear. I turned to see an older woman, perhaps fifty years old, talking to the man with the whiskers. Her face was all politeness when she smiled at her guests, but I could see lines of worry underneath… as though she was trying to hide something. They were talking in low tones, so that others could not hear, and were standing apart from the party a little. I moved towards them, carefully avoiding being passed through by more of the gathered guests.

"… and I don't see why you are insisting on this, Charles," said the woman in a low-toned and upset voice. "Charlotte is not happy with the match, and neither am I. I hear stories all over the county about Sir John… they say he is a drinker and a gambler, and there are rumours, Charles, rumours of viciousness. I do not like the thought of our daughter being wed to him. I wish you would relent."

"The decision is mine to make on whom my daughter will marry," he said stiffly, "and it has been made. Rumours follow any rich man about, and if I am not concerned about them, then you have no cause to be." He scowled over at the shape of his daughter still playing on the piano. "She is entirely too bold and will need a strong man to keep her in check," he said, bristling at his own thoughts. "I was too lenient with her as a child, doted on her too much as my only daughter. No, it is enough. Sir John will have her. He will get a fine dowry from me to take her off my hands, and she will obey me."

He turned to the woman, whose face had fallen. She was looking at her hands, her eyes hopeless. He took hold of her chin and lifted it. "It will be well, Maude," he said, almost softly, "but I will have obedience from my daughter, and from you. I am the man of this house, and I know best."

"Yes, Charles," said the woman, lifting her eyes to his. They were full of tears but she did not protest further. "I am sure you know what is right."

I was as unsure as she sounded on whether her husband was right or not. I watched with even more fascination, caught up in the story, as the day went on. I did not think to go and dress, nor go to the toilet, or any of the other things which would have made sense. I just followed these people about. I watched them gather and sit for dinner in the large dining room, and watched the face of the poor, sad girl drop as her father announced her engagement to this Sir John. He sat on the right hand side of her father; an older man, perhaps in his forties, he looked as unmatched for his potential bride as could be, smiling in a manner of smug glee which contrasted sharply with the unhappiness on the girl's face. The people at the table applauded the announcement greatly, but as I looked at the face of Charlotte, I knew that she did not.

Later, I followed poor, sad Charlotte into a parlour where there were no other people. She walked to the edge of the room and stood by a window, looking out into the darkness. She seemed entirely lost in her thoughts. I could not help but stare at her. She was so young, so pretty, and the grim set of her jaw told of tears she was trying to hold back. I thought of the life of a young woman at this time. I thought of having no right of my own to control my life, and I pitied her. My heart ached for her sadness.

For a while she just stood there, staring into the darkness, and then she thrust her shoulders back.

"You will just have to make the best of what you have," she whispered to herself. "Never mind that you hate Sir John, or that you will have to leave this house… perhaps one day, when father is gone, and the estate passes to mother under the new law, perhaps you can return…"

She looked over the dark gardens leading down to the coastal path, and I could see her mind struggling with itself. I, too, did not want to leave this house. I understood her attachment to it. But at least I was not being sold into a life I did not want… I watched her face closely as tears came to her eyes.

Then, she turned, and as she looked in my direction, she seemed to start slightly. She peered… as though she could see me. My heart thumped loud in my chest. None of the other ghosts had given any indication that they could see me at all, and now, she was staring straight at me! But, harrowing though the experience was, she stopped peering and shook her head. Then she turned and made for the door. I stood for a while in the parlour, feeling strangely more unnerved than I had done all day. Had she seen me? I had thought that she had for a moment. It took me a little while to calm down, but I followed her back out and into the throngs of the party.

I walked amongst the ghosts of the past that night; a watchful intruder who could not be seen. I watched them dance in the large parlour room, their skirts brushing the floor and their boots tapping in time with the music of the piano. I watched the mournful face of Charlotte as she talked hesitantly with the man she was being forced to marry, and I looked on the dark satisfaction of her father's face as he saw her subdued to his will. And then, as the clock struck one, the figures about me seemed to ebb and flow, waving like shadows with the coming of a light. And then, they were gone. The house remained lit; all the lights I had turned on the night before were still on. I stood in my pyjamas in the centre of the room they had used for dancing, alone, staring at the empty room.

I sat down heavily on a chair, feeling the shaking feeling of fear return to me. Or perhaps it was just the feeling of relief. For a long time I just sat there. And then, something within me made me reach for the phone. I dialled a number without hardly looking at it, and when a familiar voice answered, I said, "Hi… Simon? It's El… Look, I know it's late, but can I talk to Mum?"

*

I saw nothing more of the ghosts in the last week I stayed at the house, and strangely, despite the odd experiences of Christmas Day, I had no desire to leave the house. I had not felt threatened by the experience, and although the fate of that poor young girl, forced into a marriage she did not want with a man who was likely to turn out to be a brute made me shiver, I did not want to leave. I felt in some ways as though it had brought me closer to the house, even though that sounds insane. But it was as though I had been a part of the history of this place, an observer into the darkness of its past.

I made my peace with my mother. Perhaps it was seeing another example of a parent who had managed to overcome the wishes of his own daughter, and plunged her into a life of unhappiness which caused me to think a little less badly of my mother who could not, happily, make such choices for me. I was luckier than Charlotte... bring born into a time when I was able to make my own choices, for good or for bad... I was more fortunate than her. I pitied her, that sad, bold girl, and I wondered what had become of her in the end, forced into a life she did not want. It also gave me an odd kind of realisation of my own power. My mother might badger me and nag me, she might disapprove of my life and my ambitions, but she could not force me to do something I did not want to. The comparison of my life with the shadow of that Victorian girl gave me courage, of a strange and special kind. Charlotte had not had the choice to do what she wanted with her life, but I did, and perhaps it was even more important that I *did* what I wanted with my life, as a kind of testament to her, and every other person who had come before me, who did not have the freedom I possessed here and now.

Perhaps that was what made me make peace with my mother. I knew now that I had the courage to uphold my dreams even in the face of her disapproval, and it made me feel a little sorry for her.

"Look," I had said over the phone, sitting there alone in the brilliant light of the house on Christmas night, "I am sorry, for what I said. But I also meant some of it, Mother. You have to stop with this, this endless criticism of my life. It is *my* life, and I am going to live it as I see fit. If you can accept that, then we can be friends."

There was a huffing kind of noise down the phone. "I just…" she started, and I thought I heard a sob in her voice. "It's just… I don't want you looking back on your life, like I did, and regretting the choices that you made," she said, in a voice which threatened to break my heart. "I just want you to be *safe*, for money, for a job, and not have to scrimp and save every penny, like I used to."

"I'm sorry that you regret your choices in life, Mother," I said, feeling a little angry again, "even if that includes having me…"

"No!" she cried down the phone, "no, having you is never something I regretted… never! It was just the life I had to give you; it wasn't much compared to what your friends had…"

"I never felt as though I was missing out for a moment, Mum," I said gently, and heard her start to cry. I agreed to go and spend a couple of days with her when this job was ended. I knew that we had a lot to talk about, and we weren't going to fix everything right away, but it was a start.

Bunny and her family came back a week after the events of Christmas Day, and whilst I was showing her the house, and she was praising my skills at cleaning, saying how lovely it all looked, I mentioned that I had in fact been here on Christmas Day. She looked at me sharply, and then flushed and lowered her head.

"I saw them," I said softly, and she looked up at me.

"I'm so sorry that I didn't say…" she muttered hesitantly, trying to read the expression on my face, "it's just that some people don't see them at all, they don't experience anything… and you said that you wouldn't be here, so I thought there wouldn't be an issue… it's so hard to find good people to look after the house, and telling people something like that, well…"

"Puts them off, I understand." I smiled at her. "Please don't worry, actually, if you were willing and another opportunity came up…"

Bunny stared at me with an open mouth. "You'd… come again?" she asked. "After seeing all that?"

I nodded. "I like the house, Bunny, and the ghosts, they don't come to visit at any other time of the year, do they?" She shook her head. "Well, for the most part, I found it to be just the position I needed, right here and now, and besides," I smiled at her a little, "they made me sad, but I do not believe I fear the Christmas ghosts."

About the Author

I find people talking about themselves in the third person to be entirely unsettling, so, since this section is written by me, I will use my own voice rather than try to make you believe that another person is writing about me to make me sound terribly important.

I am an independent author, publishing my books by myself, with help on this one from the lovely Julia Gibbs, or @ProofreadJulia. I write in all the spare time I have and this year will be leaving my day-job to become a full-time author. I briefly tried entering into the realm of 'traditional' publishing but, to be honest, found the process so time consuming and convoluted that I quickly decided to go it alone and self-publish.

I mainly write historical fiction and my passion for history, in particular the era of the Tudors, began early in life. As a child I lived in Croydon, near London, and my schools were lucky enough to be close to such glorious places as Hampton Court and the Tower of London to mean that field trips often took us to those castles. My love for history, however, does not mean that I am not interested in writing other types of books, such as this one. I write as many of you read, I suspect; in many genres. My own bookshelves are weighted down with historical volumes and biographies, but they also contain dystopias, sci-fi, horror, humour, children's books, fairy tales, romance and adventure. I can't promise I'll manage to write in *all* the areas I've mentioned there, but I'd love to give it a go. If anything I've published isn't your thing, that's fine, I just hope you like the ones I write which *are* your thing! I want to divert you as readers, to please you with my writing and to have you join me on these adventures.

A book is nothing without a reader.

As to the rest of me; I am in my thirties and live in Cornwall with a rescued dog, a rescued cat and my partner (who wasn't rescued, but may well have rescued me). I studied Literature at university after I fell in love with books as a small child. When I was little I could often be found nestled half-way up the stairs with a pile of books and my head lost in another world between the pages. There is nothing more satisfying to me than finding a new book I adore, to place next to the multitudes I own and love… and nothing more disappointing to me to find a book I am willing to never open again. I do hope that this book was not a disappointment to you; I loved writing it and I hope that showed through the pages.

This is only one of a large selection of titles coming to you on Amazon. I hope you will try the others.

If you would like to contact me, please do so.

On twitter, I am @TudorTweep and am more than happy to follow back and reply to any and all messages. I may avoid you if you decide to say anything worrying or anything abusive, but I figure that's acceptable.

Via email, I am tudortweep@gmail.com a dedicated email account for my readers to reach me on. I'll try and reply within a few days.

I publish some first drafts and short stories on Wattpad where I can be found at www.wattpad.com/user/GemmaLawrence31. Wattpad was the first place I ever showed my stories, *to anyone*, and in many ways its readers and their response to my works were the influence which pushed me into independent publishing. If you have never been on the site I recommend you try it out. It's free, it's fun and it's chock-full of real emerging talent. I love Wattpad because its members and their encouragement gave me the boost I needed as a fearful waif to get some confidence in myself and make a go of a life as a real, published writer.

Thank you for taking a risk with an unknown author and reading my book. I do hope now that you've read one you'll want to read more. If you'd like to leave me a review, that would be very much appreciated also!

Gemma Lawrence
Cornwall
2016

Thank You

…to so many people for helping me make this book possible… to Julia Gibbs, my proof reader, who I worked with for the first time on this little collection of short stories, and found a delightful and diligent working-partner. To my partner Matthew, who offers support to me in my writing and manages to retain his good humour despite many, many days and weeks where he has to try to be quiet about the house as I tap away. To my family, for their ongoing love and support; this includes not only my own blood in my mother and father, sister and brother, but also their families, their partners and all my nieces who I am sure are set to take the world by storm as they grow. To Matthew's family, for their support, and for the extended family I have found myself welcomed to within theirs To all the tweeps who offered support and many retweets on Twitter for my books, and lastly, to my readers, many of whom have posted reviews of my books on Amazon and Goodreads, helping me to reach more new readers.

Thank you to all of you; you'll never know how much you've helped me, but I know what I owe to you.

Gemma
Cornwall
2016

Printed in Poland
by Amazon Fulfillment
Poland Sp. z o.o., Wrocław